"Those days are over," she whispered.

"Yes." He said it softly and took her chin tightly in his hand and kissed her gently on the mouth. "The first time I kissed you was on a cold night after the last football game of the season."

"Why are you bringing that up now?" she asked.

"I don't know. I guess you never really forget your first love." He slowly lowered his lips to hers and kissed her with slow deliberation, his lips playing, coaxing. Never had she had to fight so hard not to surrender completely, to cling to him and beg him to stay with her forever, tell him that a part of him would be with her always. With blinding clarity the truth hit her: he knew his power over her!

Dear Reader:

As the months go by, we continue to receive word from you that SECOND CHANCE AT LOVE romances are providing you with the kind of romantic entertainment you're looking for. In your letters you've voiced enthusiastic support for SECOND CHANCE AT LOVE, you've shared your thoughts on how personally meaningful the books are, and you've suggested ideas and changes for future books. Although we can't always reply to your letters as quickly as we'd like, please be assured that we appreciate your comments. Your thoughts are all-important to us!

We're glad many of you have come to associate SECOND CHANCE AT LOVE books with our butterfly trademark. We think the butterfly is a perfect symbol of the reaffirmation of life and thrilling new love that SECOND CHANCE AT LOVE heroines and heroes find together in each story. We hope you keep asking for the "butterfly books," and that, when you buy one—whether by a favorite author or a talented new writer—you're sure of a good read. You can trust all SECOND CHANCE AT LOVE books to live up to the high standards of romantic fiction you've come to expect.

So happy reading, and keep your letters coming!

With warm wishes,

Ellen Edwards

Ellen Edwards
SECOND CHANCE AT LOVE
The Berkley/Jove Publishing Group
200 Madison Avenue
New York, NY 10016

PASSION'S SONG
JOHANNA PHILLIPS

**SECOND CHANCE AT LOVE
BOOK**

For Leslie Kazanjian
for encouragement and enthusiasm...
among other things

PASSION'S SONG

Chapter

1

THIS WAS CRAZY! It had to be here, right on the end, the last space left in the plot, but the lush grass was just as smooth as if it had never been disturbed, and there was no marker that read: REBECCA LOUISE HANSON.

Nelda's heels sank into the spongy turf as she walked around the plot where her ancestors were buried. Hansens all—Hansens with an *e*. There were at least ten graves in the plot surrounded by a low stone divider. A large monument proclaimed the Hansens one of the first families to settle this rich Iowa farmland.

Her puzzled glance skimmed along the row of small headstones set in a concrete base level with the neatly manicured lawn, then swept back again to be absolutely sure what she was seeking wasn't there.

Her heart pounding like a trip-hammer, for the first time in her life Nelda doubted her sanity. She stood clutching a slender parcel of flowers while she fought for control. Hysteria began to rise in her throat, and she stared accusingly at the spot where her daughter should be buried. She choked back her fear and blinked against the glare of the sun. A weak breeze ruffled her curly dark hair and she pushed it back from her damp forehead. Her eyes clouded with bewilderment as she looked across the lawn dotted with markers toward the custodial building. At that moment a man came out the door and bent to work on a large power mower. A bluejay scolded from its perch in an evergreen tree, its squawk almost surreal in the stillness of the grove.

In a daze, Nelda walked toward the workman. She

tried to push aside the thought that she was losing her mind. Becky had to be there, in that spot! Her grandfather had given her and Lute the single plot, and her father had bought the small marker for the head of the grave. It had been a sore point with Lute to accept help when Becky died, but there had been little else he could do.

She reached the man as he wiped his hands on a greasy rag.

"Mornin', ma'am."

"Morning." Nelda was so breathless she could scarcely speak. "I'm Nelda Hanson. I'm terribly confused. My relatives are the Hansens down there"—she lifted her arm to point at the large granite monument—"the Hansens with an *e*. I haven't been back here for a long while." Tears sprang to her eyes. "She was buried in that plot, but she's gone. My daughter . . . Rebecca Louise Hanson . . . with an *o*. It would have been her birthday today."

"Well. . . ." The man continued to wipe his hands, obviously uncomfortable at witnessing the woman's distress. "Well . . . I've been workin' here five years . . . what's the name again?"

"Rebecca Louise Hanson . . . with an *o*. All the Hansens down there are spelled with an *e*. We put her there . . . she was only six months old."

"Was there a stone on the grave?"

"A small one." Nelda felt as if she were in a hollow tunnel, her own voice echoing distantly in her ears.

"Well, maybe if you looked around. . . ."

"Where else would I look!" She felt the hysteria rising again.

"Well . . ."

Her nerves vibrating at an excruciating pitch, she was sure if she had to stand before this blank face another minute she would collapse in a frenzy at the man's feet.

"All the records are down at the city office, but— wait a minute—hey, Walter!" A man wearing overalls emerged from the utility shed.

Nelda looked at the man as if he were a lifeline, her anxious eyes clinging to his weathered face.

"Know anything about a Rebecca Hanson—with an *o*—being buried down there with old Eli Hansen and his bunch?"

Sharp blue eyes raked Nelda's face. "You mean Lute Hanson's little girl?"

Nelda's heart galloped wildly. "Yes, yes. Lute's and...mine." The voice that erupted from her throat was cracked and breathy.

"Well...."

Damnit! Couldn't they say anything, but *well?* She clamped her lips shut to keep from screaming.

"Lute had her moved a long time ago."

She opened her mouth, closed it, opened it again, and gasped, "Moved? Where?" Both men stared at her.

The man in the overalls raised his arm. "Over yonder in the new part. It's been a long time—five or six years...." Nelda murmured her thanks and started walking in the direction of his pointed finger. "It's a long way," he called after her. "Clear up against the fence at the far end. Maybe you ought to drive," he finished.

His words were soon lost to Nelda as she hobbled quickly in her thin-soled sandals over the bumpy cobblestones straight down the narrow path past Sorensons, Andersons and Jacobsons—some with an *e* and some with an *o*. She vacantly noticed how well the grounds were kept, how quiet and peaceful it was, the only sound now being a mourning dove cooing its lonely call. At this end of the cemetery the walk curled around carefully plotted flowerbeds of colorful petunias backed with borders of chrysanthemums. The trees were young and vigorous, and the snowball bushes sported thick, glossy leaves.

Reaching the last section, she saw a long, low marker of dark granite with simple straight lines. It had the look of eternity about it, and carved in the stone was the name

HANSON. Nelda stumbled toward it. Two gleaming brass markers were set into the ground before it. One read: REBECCA LOUISE HANSON, *Daughter of Nelda and Lute Hanson*, followed by a date span of only six months. The other read: LUTE HANSON. Nelda thought she would faint. Lute! Then she realized that only the date of his birth was carved in the plaque; there was a blank space where the other date would be etched when he was buried here. A box overflowing with sunny yellow marigolds graced the small marker.

Nelda stood with her head bowed, feeling a strange calm replacing her panic of moments before. After a few minutes she knelt down beside the grave, lost in silent reflection. Becky would have been eight years old today, and in the second grade at school. Would her hair have been brown and curly like mine, or blond and straight like Lute's? She'd had Lute's blue eyes, and the little fuzz on the top of her head had been blond, but would it have stayed that color as she grew older? Why had Lute moved her here? Had it been such a blow to his pride to have to accept charity from her father and grandfather? But what else could they have done? Lute had been working on a farm, earning barely enough for them to get by on.

Her toes and knees cushioned in the soft grass, Nelda realized she was gently cradling the gladiolus—the only pink flowers the florist had had—still swathed in their protective green tissue paper. Tentatively peeling away the wispy layers, she saw that the stems of the flowers were too long for the delicate marble urn that flanked the brass marker. She dug into her shoulder bag to find a nail file. Sawing away with the crude cutting tool, her thoughts coursing in a million directions and her senses absorbed in her task, she was unaware there was anyone nearby until she saw the large, scuffed jogging shoes and the legs of faded jeans.

A swift spasm shook her frame, and mechanically she

rose, moving like someone in a dream. She felt every drop of blood in her body drain to her toes. Her eyes riveted on the man standing silently on the other side of her child's grave. Shocked speechless, she opened her mouth in a swift intake of breath.

Lute? Could this big, muscular man be the lean, lanky boy she had married when she was seventeen and he was nineteen? Somehow she knew it was, despite the blond mustache on his upper lip and the hair that was trimmed to cover the tips of his ears. Mirrored sunglasses covered his eyes, but she knew they would be pale, bright blue, and startling in their intensity. He was bare-headed, and his thick, blond hair glistened in the dazzling sunlight. His shoulders looked a yard wide in the tight knit shirt. In one large hand was a small wreath of fresh flowers.

The silence pounded against Nelda's ears as her eyes drank in his form. Straining to initiate a normal greeting despite the chaos raging in her brain, she barely managed a whispered, "Hello, Lute."

There was silence. When he continued to just stand there staring, saying nothing, she had to stifle the wild impulse to reach out and touch him, to somehow verify his physical presence. Finally he said, "What brought you back?"

She lifted her shoulders, trying to encompass a world of explanations with the silent gesture. She wished he would take off the sunglasses so she could read his expression, but all she could see was a reflection of her own distress.

"Why did you move her?" she asked, startled by her own bluntness.

"Why not?" he replied evenly, as if she'd posed the most commonplace question in the world. "She was my daughter. As soon as I had the money, I bought a plot of ground and buried her in it."

Even his voice was deeper and stronger than she remembered. This man didn't remotely resemble the long-haired, soft-spoken boy who had insisted on standing beside her when she informed her horrified parents she was four months pregnant.

"You could have notified me."

"I would have if I'd . . . thought you were interested." His momentary hesitation was quickly displaced by an almost fierce firmness.

"How can you say that?" she asked haltingly.

"I say it because you didn't even share your grief with me. I, too, had lost a child—a part of myself!" His face was suddenly harsh and powerful, the jaw jutted in angry determination, the mouth curved downward reflecting his contempt for her.

"You froze me out, Lute," she said accusingly. Relived anguish tore into her heart. "Of course I grieved alone. You didn't even cry!"

"How do you know? Just because I didn't make a big show of tears for your family doesn't mean I didn't sorrow for my little girl. You barely communicated with me in those days anyway. You didn't need me, Nelda. I was merely the instrument that made you pregnant. Your folks considered me poor white trash and started easing me out of your life the day we were married. And you let them!"

Stunned at his outburst and grasping in a flash of sudden clarity how badly they'd misread each other's withdrawal, Nelda sprang to the defense.

"That's not how it was at all! I just wanted us to go back to school. You know how I'd always hoped to become a decorator, and I wanted for you to learn something besides farming. Daddy would have lent you the money."

"And what's wrong with farming?" He whipped the sunglasses from his face, and his blue eyes pinned hers. "I told you when we married that I wouldn't take a dime from your folks. I was forced to when Becky died, but just as soon as I could manage I moved her to a plot of ground *I* paid for, and I sent your father a check for the original marker. I don't suppose he told you about that!" He was looking at her as if he despised her. "You were ashamed of what I could afford for you," he said tightly, his lips curved in what looked like a sneer. "The only things I could give you were Becky and an *o* in your name. When Becky died it was a good excuse to get rid of the family embarrassment, so you let them take you off to Florida. I didn't desert you, Nelda. You deserted me!"

Nelda almost reeled from the force of his bitterness. His words hit her like stones. She knew her face whitened, and she looked away from him. Her gaze fell on the grave of their child, and all the sweet, bitter memories came rushing back.

Never, not even if she lived a million years, she thought, would she be as happy as she'd been during the first few months of their marriage. Lute had been a tender, possessive lover who was as hungry for affection as she was. He had worked hard, putting in long hours as a farm laborer, but once Becky was born his earnings had barely covered the necessities, let alone any luxuries. She had wanted more for him, wanted his life to be easier, and she had urged him to let her father finance his schooling. Only later had she realized that Lute could never be anything except what he was—a fiercely independent personality who refused to fit into the mold her father offered.

During the later months—after they'd lost Becky— they had lost each other, too. He had become quiet and withdrawn, a person she scarcely knew, and she was too overwhelmed by her own heartbreak—and maybe just too immature—to cope with his moods. It had hurt bitterly when he refused to go south with her, but she had bowed to her parents' arguments about leaving the past behind and had gone. A few months after she'd settled into school there, her father had insisted that she see a

divorce lawyer. Despite her parents' convictions, she had
held out the hope that Lute would come to her, that their
love was strong enough to persuade him to give up his
dream of owning a farm. But he'd signed the divorce
papers, and she had tried to reconcile herself to the fact
that their time together was over.

"Are you trying to make me feel guilty, Lute?" Fairly
quivering with torment, Nelda looked at him. "I've never
blamed you for anything. Even at sixteen I knew the risk
we were taking when we made love. I never regretted it
for one second. You and Becky were my life. For the
first time I had something of my very own, something
my parents hadn't bought for me." Tears filled her eyes
and she tried to blink them away.

Not since Becky died had she felt such crushing anguish. She wanted to hate him for being here, for bringing
back the heartache she had tried so hard to overcome,
but hate wouldn't come. Instead, she remembered his
tenderness when she told him she was pregnant, and how
he had held her and promised to love her and take care
of her for the rest of his life. A big promise for a skinny
boy of nineteen with only a widowed mother for a family.

Lute seemed to study her carefully—to be looking
deeply into her eyes—but she couldn't read the emotions
flashing across his features. For a moment she thought
he was on the verge of tears, but then he was down on
his knees, his fingers raking some dead grass away from
the marker and carefully placing his floral wreath. Through
a blur of unshed tears Nelda watched his capable movements. She remained standing, the full weight of what
was happening holding her in place. She saw the sun
glisten off the blond hairs on his forearms, and her gaze
traveled down to his hands. The glint of a wedding ring
caught her eyes. Lute had remarried! A wave of sickness
surged through her.

*Lute! Oh, Lute, with the wind-blown hair and the sun-
browned neck, where did our love go? Do you ever think*

of that time, so long ago, when we couldn't be near each other without touching, and when our eyes would cling to each other, even across a crowded room? We had to be together every possible minute in those days. I remember, my first love, how my body sang for you. . . .

Lute abruptly stood and looked down at her, his face shuttered once more. She instantly dropped her gaze to the gladiolus.

"You'll need water for those. I'll get some." He pried his hand into his jeans pocket and brought out a jackknife. "Here. You can cut the stems with this," he offered, almost gently, it seemed.

Nelda took the tool from his hand without looking at him and knelt down to work on the flowers still lying spread on the waxy florist paper. Her fingers were shaking and she could hardly open the knife, but she managed and automatically began to cut the stems. Her mind was still in an eddy of confusion when she finished and bunched the flowers in the marble vase.

Lute returned and poured a generous amount of water from a coffee can into both the box of blooming marigolds and her vase. Without a word he took the knife from her hand, picked up the stem ends she had cut, and dropped them into the can.

When he stood again, Nelda blurted, "I didn't remember that you were so tall."

"I've done a lot of growing during the past eight years, both in mind and in body. A man grows up fast when his wife packs up and leaves him."

During this clipped speech Nelda stood quietly, only her eyes moving, looking quickly away from him and back again.

"I wanted you to come with us to Florida," she said, returning to her argument.

"And accept handouts from your old man?" he rejoined. "No way! I'd already had enough of his charity. Face the truth, Nelda—if you'd wanted our marriage to last, you would have stayed with me." She could tell he was getting angry again, but his voice remained calm.

"Can't you understand how depressed I was? Lute, I was only seventeen!"

"Old enough to have a baby, to make a home . . . for a while." He paused, a pained expression crossing his face. "Old enough to sue for divorce," he added, his words like icicles being snapped to pieces.

"Daddy said you wanted nothing more to do with me."

"You could have found out for yourself what I wanted. But it's over now, done and forgotten." He flung the last words over his shoulder and walked rapidly toward the black pickup truck parked in the lane.

Nelda looked down at the grave one last time and started across the cemetery. She felt as if all the strength had been drained out of her, but she stiffened her back and held her head erect.

Lute put the can into the back of the truck and stood beside the door until she reached him. "How did you get out here?"

"My car is over there . . . where I thought Becky would be."

"Get in. I'll drive you over. You look as if you're about to drop."

Nelda hesitated, wilting in the oppressive heat. "Thanks. I'd appreciate a lift."

By the time she reached the passenger side of the truck Lute had flung open the door. It was a high step into the cab, but she grabbed the door handle and pulled herself up. It had been years since she'd been in a pickup truck, and then never one as nice as this one with its red leather seats and plush black carpeting on the floorboards. She thought of the battered old pickup Lute used to drive when they were going together. They'd driven that old truck to their favorite picnic spot, where they had made love for the very first time. She rushed into speech, not wanting to remember.

"Is your mother well?"

"Fine. Yours?"

"Mama died five years ago."

"I'm sorry to hear that," he responded slowly, and she wondered if it was concern she heard in his voice.

"Daddy has remarried. They live in Florida," she hurried on.

"I heard your grandparents went there, too."

"They did, but Grandpa only lived a short while. Grandma stayed. She knew she couldn't live on the homestead alone, but she had Mr. Hutchinson keep it up just the same. She died last winter."

"I'd heard about your grandparents. A real shame. I liked them both—they were real decent."

Yes, she thought. You fit in with my earthy grandparents, but you and my parents were at loggerheads from the moment you met. I was constantly torn between you. She wondered only fleetingly how he'd heard about Gran and Grandpa.

"Is that your car?"

"Yes, the one with the U-Haul. Oh no, I forgot about Kelly! I bet he's dying for a drink." Disregarding Lute's quizzical glance, Nelda popped out of the pickup and hurried to her car to let the panting Irish setter out. "I'm sorry, boy. I forgot it would be so hot in there." Kelly shot out the door and, nose to the ground, explored the immediate vicinity.

Nelda heard the truck door slam, then saw Lute getting the coffee can from the back. She thought he had an odd expression on his face before he called out, "Come on, boy. Let's get you a drink."

Kelly happily bounded after Lute across the lawn to a marble water fountain, then greedily lapped water from the can Lute proferred. Nelda watched them, hardly believing it was Lute who was there with her dog. Lute. In all her dreams she had never imagined that he was anything but an older version of that thin, blue-eyed boy with the shy smile. Discovering that he was now a virile, rugged, terribly handsome man sent her already confused senses into a reeling revolution.

When the pair returned, Lute dropped the can back into the truck and stood staring at her, looking like he was about to speak. Instead, he turned and got into the cab, immediately starting the engine.

Stunned by his abruptness, Nelda managed a brief, "Thanks, Lute."

"Headed for the old homestead?" he tossed out casually. At her nodded assent, he raised his hand in salute and drove off.

Nelda watched until the black truck passed between the stone pillars, then got into her car and called to Kelly, thinking that Lute hadn't even asked how long she'd be here. Automatically she put the Olds into gear and pulled out onto the highway, following that to the country blacktop and then turning north on a graveled road. All attempts to put Lute from her mind were meeting with resistance. She kept seeing the ring on his finger. *I gave him a wedding ring, a narrow gold band much like the one he was wearing.* What type of woman had he chosen for his wife? Oh, God! Why should it hurt after all these years to picture him with someone else? When she was in New York she often thought of him, but always as he had been—and on his own. And not a day passed that she wasn't reminded that she had given birth to his daughter. A child playing in the street, an advertisement in a magazine, or a program on television always pulled that memory sharply into focus. For a long time the pain of remembering Becky had been powerful enough to double her over, but gradually she was able to recall the pleasures of motherhood as well. She sometimes wondered if she'd ever experience those pleasures again.

After her father had told her that Lute was anxious to be free of her, she had tried to close her mind to him, to pick up the threads of her life, and, by keeping busy, to hold thoughts of him at bay. Now the magic, the inexplicable magnetism of him, was eating at her, making contentment impossible. Somehow she'd always felt she would see him again. She'd recognized she would have to—to purge him, once and for all, from her thoughts. But now, on her first day back here, he had come barreling into her life again, blasting all her cool philosophizing. And he was married to another. Her heartbeat escalated, her palms grew moist, and a dull ache settled in the middle of her body.

Nelda turned the Oldsmobile pulling the U-Haul trailer into a lane and approached a sign that announced: 4-H MEMBER LIVES HERE.

"Not anymore, huh, Kelly?" she observed tiredly, fondling the dog's ears. "We'll have to put up a new sign. One that says: POOPED INTERIOR DESIGNER AND KELLY LIVE HERE." The setter nuzzled her arm and looked up at her with soulful eyes.

The house was set back from the road on a grassy knoll bordered on the north by a thick grove of cedars and on the west by a cornfield. East of the house she spied a rambling hedge of lilac bushes. Nelda feasted her eyes on the white frame, two-story house with the glassed in front porch and the long-paned windows they were nearing. Some of the most pleasant times of her childhood had been spent here with her grandparents.

She was exhausted from her long drive from New York, but the trip had helped her unwind from her last job of creating a totally new décor for one of New York's most exclusive nightclubs.

Now she was home. Home? How long had she been thinking of Iowa as home, she mused.

It had been years since she'd been here. She'd forgotten how hot and sultry it was, and how high the country roads were graded so the snow could blow off and into the ditches on each side. She'd also forgotten how tall the corn grew. It was beyond her understanding how corn could be knee-high by July fourth—a farmer's standard for a good crop—and be well over six feet tall by the middle of August.

August in Iowa was fair time, too. As she'd driven though Mason City she'd seen acres of cars and stock trailers parked at the fair grounds. The ferris wheel was spinning and spangled pennants were fluttering from the grandstand where the rodeo was being held. Ten years ago she would have been there, holding tightly to Lute's arm as they strolled toward the cattle barns. Lute had loved to hang around the stock pens, looking at the champion stock and talking to the boys who were exhibiting them.

Lute. How long ago it had been! She could scarcely think of it being herself in that other life.

The car bumped over the rutted lane, the trailer jiggling along behind. Nelda pulled around behind the house and parked alongside the back porch, like Grandpa used to do. She sat in the car and looked out over the yard. It had been neatly mowed and the bushes trimmed. A piece of heavy rope—all that remained of the swing Grandpa had made—hung from the big elm tree. She was glad to see her friendly giant had survived the Dutch Elm disease that had swept this part of the country several years ago. It was standing as sturdy as ever, but somehow it didn't seem as huge as it had when she'd looked up at it as a child.

"We're home, Kelly," she said softly.

The dog scrambled out of the car, promptly dipping his nose to the ground to sniff all the new, exciting smells. As she climbed the concrete steps to the back door, Nelda fumbled in her purse for the key her Grandpa's lawyer had sent her.

She soon stood in the middle of the kitchen and looked around the familiar room. She smiled when she spotted the microwave oven—Grandma's one concession to "modern conveniences." Everything was clean, the tile floor shining, the windows sparkling. When she had called her Grandpa's lawyer, Mr. Hutchinson, from New York and told him she was on the way, he had assured her the house would be ready for occupancy and all she had to do was bring her personal belongings and stock the refrigerator.

Nelda went to the door and called Kelly in before she inspected the rest of the house. Enraptured by the natural scents of grass and trees and warm earth, the dog took his sweet time responding to her whistle.

"You're a city mutt," she scolded as he trailed into the house. "You'd better stay inside until I can go out with you. No telling what you'll get into out there."

His tail between his legs, Kelly looked adequately chastened, sulking like a disappointed child. He definitely wasn't happy to be in the house. He pressed his wet nose against the clean window pane and looked out, something he couldn't manage in their high-rise apartment in New York.

"Look at it this way, dog. We'll be here for at least six months. You'll have plenty of time to explore the countryside. So come on, wag your tail and let me know you're happy that I'll have time to work on my designs."

Kelly's tail made a halfhearted wag, then he turned back to gaze with longing at the grove of thick evergreens and underbrush.

The steady hum told her that the refrigerator was running. Her first trip to the car was to pick up the two sacks of groceries she'd bought at the supermarket in Mason City after she'd driven past the high school and then her old home. It hadn't looked like the same place. The house that had once been her mother's pride and joy was now painted a muddy brown and appeared to be a two-family dwelling.

She'd also driven slowly past the small apartment house where she and Lute had lived during the short time they were married. Catching a glimpse of colorful curtains in the window of what had once been their bedroom, she'd remembered with a pang how she'd frugally decorated it herself, sewing drapes and slipcovers and refurbishing secondhand furniture to stay within their budget. She'd known her mother disapproved, but she'd also realized that Lute was secretly pleased with the cozy home she'd created.

Humble beginnings for her recent commercial success, she reflected fondly. After her formal education, she'd moved to New York and established herself firmly in the field of interior design. Her last job had cemented her status among commercial decorators, and had more than left her solvent for a while. Yes, this was the ideal time to take a leave of absence and pursue an unfulfilled dream of trying her hand at textile design, and Grandma's house was the perfect retreat. And only by coming here, she reasoned, could she make a decision about whether or not to sell the farm her grandparents had left her. Then too, always in the back of her mind was the picture of Lute, her first love. She'd had to see him again if she was ever going to break loose from her past, be content with her solitary life, or find happiness with someone else.

By the time Nelda finished the unloading her back hurt, two of her long, beautiful nails were broken, and her shirt was glued to her body with sweat. She tried to run her fingers through her hair, but it was damp and kinked beyond control. Grimacing, she remembered the years when she'd wanted it long and straight and had coaxed her mother to allow her to have it straightened in the style her friends were wearing. Now it was cut short and, to her, resembled a curly metal pad used to scrub pots and pans. She finally made her way to the bathroom off the kitchen—converted from a pantry so necessary to the houses of eighty years ago. It was certainly roomy, and its charming, old-fashioned fixtures included an oak commode with a towel bar across the top. Peeling off her sodden clothes, she filled the claw-footed bathtub with warm water and eased her slender frame down into it.

Kelly nosed open the door and padded into the room. He tilted his head and looked inquiringly at Nelda.

"It's a far cry from the sunken tub in the apartment, isn't it, fella? But we'll get used to it. And all that peace and quiet out there is going to be a blessing for both of us, Kelly. I hadn't realized how easy it is to lose sight of goals in the hustle and bustle of the city. Here I'll have plenty of time to rest and think and decide what direction my life should take now."

As she heard her enthusiastic words echo falsely off the tiled walls, she wondered if her grand plans would prove as ephemeral as the soap bubbles collapsing weakly into the cooling bath water. Now that Lute was married. . . .

Chapter

2

NELDA WORKED AS if possessed. One day, to her total amazement, she saw that the boxes she had thought would take forever to unpack were empty, folded flat, and stored in the shed. Her books were arranged on the long oak library table in the living room, the stereo was set up with a speaker cord tacked neatly along the stairway baseboard to bring music to her upstairs bedroom, and her workbench and supplies were in place on the glassed in front porch. And she'd already begun gathering the plants, leaves, and wildflowers she planned to use as patterns for her designs. Her aching muscles attested to the fact that she alone was responsible for these minor miracles.

By that night she was so tired she bathed and got ready for bed without even listening to the evening news— something she never missed in New York. "Dumb old thing," she muttered at the blank television screen before heading upstairs to the haven of the four-poster walnut bed. "I almost ruptured myself getting you into the house. I doubt if you're worth it."

Waking early the next morning out of the deep sleep of the righteously weary, she listened to the school bus rumble past the house before she jumped out of bed to attack a new day. Her enthusiasm flagged momentarily as the image of a tousle-haired, sleepy-eyed Lute danced into her head and scattered the remnants of her recent dreaming. Stretching vigorously, she worked to tone her body and strengthen her mind against the disturbing invasion. Glancing out the window at the sun-drenched day, she suddenly realized that, except for a couple of trips to the supermarket, she'd been so absorbed in settling in that she hadn't left the place for quite some time. She'd laid in a huge supply of dog food for Kelly, but for the most part she was subsisting on an occasional bowl of soup or a baked potato from the microwave. Hardly the proper way to keep her energy flowing, she chided herself.

The only blot on her peaceful existence—other than her nagging thoughts of Lute—was the motorcycle that passed the house several times a week. Kelly detested motorcycles, and on the long trip from New York he had growled and snapped his teeth at each and every one they'd encountered. Whenever this one sped past he raced through the house barking furiously. "Hush," Nelda scolded each time. "That bike has nothing to do with you. Calm down." She regarded the dog now peacefully sunning himself on the back steps. No demons for either of them today, she resolved.

Plotting to leave her afternoon free for an inspirational walk through the countryside and a return to her workbench with fresh ideas, Nelda began making her preparations. Pleased that she'd thought to pick up a roast on her last shopping trip and thaw it in the refrigerator overnight, she took it out and began liberally seasoning it. She hated cooking for just herself, but reasoned that she could have some of the beef hot for lunch and then eat off it for the next few days. Still, she couldn't help thinking how much more gratifying it would be to be preparing this for . . . someone else.

Cursing her errant thoughts, she popped the roast into the preheated oven and skipped upstairs to strip her bed. Returning to gather the towels from the bathroom, she began her small washload. When the washing machine buzzer sounded she was standing in the kitchen gazing out the porch door and admiring the shimmer of the leafy elm branches in the brisk summer breeze. Suddenly re-membering the fresh, outdoorsy scent of line-dried bed-ding from her childhood days at Grandma's house, she decided to forego the convenience of the electric dryer and hauled the basket of wet laundry to the clothesline. She wiped off the line and pinned up the two sheets. She was just starting on the towels when she heard the dreaded roar of the motorcycle. Frantically she looked about for Kelly. He was standing beside the house, his head cocked to one side, the fur on the back of his neck standing at attention.

"Kelly! No!" Nelda knew as she shouted that it would do no good. She dropped the towels into the basket and took off in a run after the red streak tearing down the lane toward the road. "Kel—ly! Kel—ly! Come back here!"

Kelly reached the road, whirling and barking at the machine coming toward him. He lunged and jumped, his own barks drowning out the voice of his mistress calling him. For a moment Nelda thought he'd turn tail and run, but instead he dashed back directly into the path of the machine. He flew into the air, landed hard, and lay still. The rider had done his best to avoid the collision, the back wheel of the cycle spinning in the gravel before the machine went skidding down the incline into the ditch beside the road.

Nelda stood with her hands over her ears, her heart pounding like the beat of a drum. Oh, no! Oh God, no! She began to run again. Her frightened eyes saw the rider limp up out of the ditch. Thank God, he was all right, but Kelly . . . he lay like a limp, red blanket in the road.

The man reached the dog at the same time Nelda did. She threw herself onto her knees. "Oh, Kelly, don't be . . ." With relief she saw that he was still breathing. He whined and tried to lift his head. In anguish, Nelda cried, "Do something, can't you? It's all your fault."

The man unfastened the chin strap and lifted the visored helmet from his head.

"Lute!" The blond hair was plastered with sweat and the blue eyes so narrowed she couldn't see them. He bent over the dog. "Do something. Oh, please, do something."

He looked at her and then back at Kelly, who was weakly emitting pitiful yelps.

"Get your car and a blanket to put him on. We'll take him to the vet," he issued crisply.

"Will he be all right?" She hated to ask the question, but she had to know. The dog had been her companion for the past five years; to lose him would be unbearable.

"I don't know. He's been stunned badly. Get moving."

Nelda ran to the house, grabbed a blanket, snatched up her purse, turned the lock on the door and slammed it. Once in the car she fumbled for the keys. She whipped the car into gear, backed it up, and turned it around. Her breath was coming in gasps. She had run so fast she had a pain in her side, but she ignored it.

She saw Lute wheel the cycle up out of the ditch and park it in the yard beside the lilacs. When she stopped the car, he reached for the blanket and spread it over the back seat. Nelda jumped from the car and knelt beside the dog, who looked up at her with pleading eyes, bringing tears to her own.

"You'll be all right," she crooned. "You just forgot that you're a city dog and not used to running free." She rubbed the back of her hand over her eyes to rid them of tears before she looked at Lute.

"I'll try not to hurt him when I lift him," he murmured. "Hold the door open. Easy now, fella. I know this is going to hurt, but we'll do it as fast as we can and get you to the vet. He'll have you fixed up in no time." Kelly let out a yelp and tried to move his back legs when Lute burrowed his hands beneath his body. "Whoa, fella. Easy now." Lute spoke in a low soothing voice, lifting the dog in his arms and easing him onto the blanket-covered seat. "You ride back here with him and try to keep him quiet," he instructed Nelda. Obediently she climbed in beside Kelly, and Lute closed the door.

Loose gravel noisily spattered the fenders as Lute drove the big car swiftly down the road. Nelda stroked Kelly's head, praying he was not seriously injured. She thanked God it was Lute who'd hit him, not some uncaring stranger who would have simply driven off. She looked up in gratitude at the sun-streaked blond head before her, an unbidden thought invading her mind. *Oh, Lute! I remember when my hands knew every inch of your body, and yours knew mine.* As if she had spoken, blue eyes met hers in the rearview mirror, and Lute's intense stare brought color flooding to her face.

"It's just a mile or so now." His words broke the spell. "Let's hope Gary is home. This is calf judging day at the fair; he could be over there." Lute met Nelda's panic stricken eyes in the mirror again. "If he isn't home, we can run over to the fair grounds; it's only a fifteen-minute drive," he added reassuringly.

By the time they turned into a drive and pulled up in front of a brick building set close to a new ranch-style house, Kelly was lying quietly, his eyes closed, his mouth open, and his long tongue hanging limply out the side of it.

"I'll see if Gary's here." Lute spoke quietly but moved quickly.

Nelda watched him try the office door. It was locked, and her heart sank to her toes. He strode briskly to the house and rang the doorbell. Despite her anguish over Kelly, Nelda couldn't take her eyes off Lute. He had the most magnificent physique she had ever seen. His shoulders, hugged by a knit shirt, were broad and muscular, his waist and hips small. His jeans molded to his thighs as if he had put them on wet and let them dry. No words would come to her mind to describe him. She had loved him once for all his tender, caring qualities when he was young. Now here he was again, all gentleness and compassion, the way she remembered him before their harsh words in the cemetery. But the hardness in his eyes that day—and the hardness of his muscular body now—belied those youthful memories. What had really happened to change him so? And why did she still hear her heart singing out for him?

She tugged her attention back to the wounded dog, and within moments Lute returned and opened the door. She looked up at him hopefully.

"Gary will open the office."

A tall, thin man in cut-off jeans and running shoes came into view behind Lute.

"Gary, this is Nelda," Lute said, extending his hand to help her out of the car.

"Nelda," he murmured thoughtfully. "Nelda?" The man's eyes flew to Lute, then back to her. "Well, hello, dear lady. Let's see what we can do for your beastie here. Lute says he ran him down with that blasted cycle of his."

"It wasn't Lute's fault," Nelda defended quickly, her hand still tingling from Lute's touch. "Kelly hasn't been in the country before. He's only been outside off a leash a few times in his life. It's hard for him to cope with all this freedom."

"I'll get a stretcher out of the office and we'll get him onto the table." He fondled Kelly's ears. "That's a good beastie. Just hang in there, old boy, and we'll see what's to be done with you."

Gary unlocked the office door and disappeared inside.

"Oh, Lute! What did he mean?" Her lips trembled. She was torn between her anxiety for Kelly and the heady experience of being with Lute. Her eyes clung to his face.

"Don't worry. Gary's a good vet—the best." His voice was gentle and reassuring. "Even if he is an Englishman," he amended in a loud stage whisper.

"I heard that, Lute. One more disparaging remark and I'll bloody well castrate that bull of yours when I come out to vaccinate him tomorrow." Gary positioned a stretcher beside the car. "Get to the other side, and we'll lift him out on the blanket and slide him onto the board. Righto, out you get, old boy."

Nelda sat in the waiting room, too nervous to even thumb through the magazines there. She had wanted to go into the treatment room with Kelly, but Lute had shaken his head and guided her to a chair.

"It's best you stay here. I'll go in with him. Relax, you look worn out."

It wasn't until she was seated that she thought about his words. How natural it seemed to have him with her. And how many times in the past had he told her that she was wearing herself out? It had been a long time since anyone had been so solicitous of her. In New York, the regimen of her job had prevented her from making many strong attachments.

Oh, heavens! The thought suddenly struck her that Lute might have a family, a son or a daughter—a sturdy little blond-haired boy, or a dainty little blue-eyed girl. She felt the panic build. Now that she'd seen him, and still felt what she was feeling, the thought of meeting his children—Becky's little half-brother or sister—tied her stomach into knots.

"Don't look so terrified," Lute was beside her, his voice gentle. "Gary says Kelly has a few cracked ribs and some paralysis in his back legs, but that he'll probably fully recover."

Nelda got unsteadily to her feet. "Oh! Thank God. And thank you, Lute. I was so scared. Kelly's really a very smart dog. He understands most of what I say to him, but he gets a little crazy when he hears a motorcycle." She had rushed into breathless speech.

Lute smiled tolerantly at her. "He won't be chasing any more motorcycles. I can almost guarantee it, but just to make sure, I won't ride by the house for a while."

"It was you all the time?"

"I haven't seen many bikes in the area other than mine. I usually take a spin out that way several times a week. Come on in and talk to Gary."

His hand was beneath her elbow as he ushered her into the treatment room. He didn't remove it, and she was grateful for his support. The room smelled of disinfectant and was stark and bare. Her precious Kelly lay still on the table.

"My wife took the kids over to watch the calf judging," Gary began conversationally as soon as she entered the room. "She'll want to meet you. She's a great crusader, my Rhetta. She'll try to rope you in on her bloody projects." He was drying his hands on a towel, his dark eyes intent on her and Lute. He was an attractive man, long and lean, with dark hair, dark eyes, and a coal black beard. Nelda warmed to him instantly. They reviewed Kelly's problems, then he gave her some medication, and she prepared to leave.

With Kelly sedated and ensconced on the blanket in the back seat once again, Gary completed his instructions. "When he comes to, he may vomit. If he'll eat, wrap one of these in a piece of ground meat or his favorite dog food and he'll sleep the night. After I go out to Lute's tomorrow, I'll stop by; that is, if that blasted bull of his hasn't gored me to death. Ring me up if you have any problems before that." His eyes twinkled at Lute, but he was firmly closing the car's back door and opening the front so Nelda could get in on the passenger side. "I'm expecting to be fed well tomorrow, Lute—crumpets, biscuits, and all at teatime. And are you quite sure you'll not forget the cucumber sandwiches?" he teased.

"It costs damn near as much to feed you, you hollow-legged cow-quack, as it does to pay your bills!" Lute growled playfully as he held out his hand. "Thanks, Gary. See you tomorrow."

He slid in under the steering wheel. There was no doubt that Lute was going to be the one to drive the Oldsmobile back to the farmhouse.

Nelda didn't speak until they were out on the highway. "Will he know where to find me?"

Lute looked at her then, and in the small confines of the car his eyes caught and held hers.

"I like your hair that way," he commented, ignoring her question. "It suits you better than long and straight." He seemed to say the words against his will. He turned his head quickly back to the road, and she gazed at his profile. His hair tumbled over his forehead in disorder; his nose was straight and finely chiseled. The mustache was what made him look so virile, she decided. She wondered what it would be like to kiss him again. A longing to touch him started in her lips, which parted softly, and slowly enveloped her. She sucked in her stomach against the sensation, turning and leaning over the seat to stroke Kelly's ears.

"Everyone in five townships knows that Severt Hansen's granddaughter is back living in the home place," he said abruptly, reverting to her question as if nothing else had been spoken. She regretted his withdrawal into the impersonal, but rewarded his surprising comment with a wide-eyed stare. "Not much happens around here, you know. That would be big news," he offered simply in the face of her confusion.

"How strange. I've only had one visitor—Ervin Olson. What a nice man. He pulled into the lane the other morning and stopped to talk for a few minutes. I thought he'd appointed himself a welcome wagon of one—or a square-dance recruiter, one or the other." She laughingly recounted how the snowy-haired widower had asked if she'd like to join him and his "lady friend" at their square-dance group one evening. His polite formality combined with his striped overalls had reminded her of her grandfather. "The one thing Grandpa hated about Florida was that Gran didn't let him wear overalls," she concluded.

Lute chuckled. "Well, now you know Ervin's the best newspaper we have, once he gets his crops in."

They rode along in silence. There were many things Nelda wanted to ask him, but she didn't dare steer the conversation into a personal channel. *Oh, Lute, Lute! Tell me about yourself. Tell me every little detail of what you've been doing,* her thoughts begged, even as her eyes returned to him again and again.

"How long will you be here?" he asked as he turned into the graveled road.

"I don't know for sure. I'd planned to spend the winter, but now . . . I don't know."

"Tired of country life already?" There was a new tone in his voice, and it hurt.

"Oh, no. I love it. I always did love it at Gran's. You know that." He glanced at her, and her eyes followed his down to the cleavage revealed by her partially unbuttoned shirt. Her hand automatically moved to fasten the wayward button. Had she wanted to say anything else, it would have been impossible. She looked straight ahead, conscious of the head that turned toward her often now that they were on the little-used road. Once she turned and gazed back into his eyes, so astonishingly blue in his tanned face. She began to feel uncomfortable. She knew her skin was flushed with color, and that the humid warmth had made a curly mop of her hair. Dimly she registered that her jeans were soiled, her shirt limp.

"Nelda . . ." The sound of her name coming from his lips made her heart lurch. "You never did say why you came back. I'd think it pretty tame around here for you."

She pulled her bottom lip through her teeth several times and stared straight ahead. "I guess you would think that," she said slowly. "But I can sum it up in a few words. I got tired of the rushing, the noise, the back-biting dog-eat-dog business of commercial decorating. I had a very successful year, so I thought I'd come back to the farm and decide if I wanted to sell it or not. I also want to try my hand at a craft I haven't had time for before."

She waited for a sarcastic reply, but Lute didn't speak until they reached the house. He drove into the back yard and parked the car under the elm tree.

"You'd better have that garage cleaned out so you can get the car into it this winter."

Her legs were trembling when she got out of the car. She started toward the house to open the door for Kelly, then remembered that the house keys were on the ring with the car keys. She turned back and ran full tilt into Lute, who had moved to open the back door of the car. His hands shot out and steadied her. Her thighs and hips were against his, and she jumped back as if he were scalding hot.

"Oh, sorry. I—I need the keys."

Still holding onto her arm with one hand, he reached into the car and pulled them from the ignition. His eyes dropped to her blouse, and she flushed hotly. Ever since his first glance, she had been self-consciously aware of her breasts left unrestrained beneath the cotton shirt. Now the damp fabric clung and her nipples stood out prominently.

She took the keys from him, and when she moved away, his hand fell from her arm.

"Are you going to put him on the porch or in the house?" His voice sounded perfectly natural, but her poise had vanished and she croaked out her words.

"The house."

"I'll carry him in then. You'd better lay some papers; he won't be able to go out for a while."

Nelda escaped to the house. His power to completely disarm her frightened her, yet it thrilled her, too. Right now she felt a tingling sensation in her thighs. No man—and she had been in contact with many on her assignments this past year—had ever made her quiver and long to be touched like this man did. Oh, damn, damn! Why couldn't he have just turned into a balding, pot-bellied red-neck she could have dismissed from her thoughts at first sight?

Lute carried the groggy dog into the kitchen and gently placed him on the floor.

"I thought he'd be cooler if he lay on the tile. You should have an air conditioner. It's like an oven in here."

"Oven! Oh, I forgot my roast!" She hurried to the stove and pulled open the oven door. The light came on and she saw the small dark brown roast lying in the sea of juices. "It isn't ruined!" she spouted with surprised relief. She turned to look over her shoulder at Lute. He was standing on spread legs, his hands wedged in the back pockets of his jeans, something close to a smile on his face. Happiness suddenly filled her and she smiled. "I'm not much of a cook," she acknowledged.

"I remember," he said softly. "Here, let me get the pan out and you can turn the oven off." He took a towel from the counter and lifted the roaster to the top of the stove. He looked around. "No wonder it's hot in here. All the windows are closed."

"I couldn't open them. They're stuck. It must be the humidity."

"This type of storm window stays on, and the bottom slides up," he explained as he twisted the hook on the top of one window sash, effortlessly lifted the window, and reached out to slide up the outer pane and pull down the screen. "This winter you'll slide the screen up again and lower the storm."

"I know how they operate, but I wondered how in the world I was going to get at them if I couldn't open the inside windows." She was talking to Lute's back, trying to ignore the fluttering of her heart. He was moving through the house raising the stuck windows. "It's cooler already. I had to prop open the front and back doors to get the smoke from my first cooking disaster out of the house. Oh, Lute! Smell that fresh country air!" Nelda knew she was babbling as she followed him from room to room, but she couldn't seem to stop.

"All I can smell is that roast in there," he growled as he strained to lift a tight window that had been closed for years. Fascinated, she watched the muscles rippling across his shoulderblades. "There's not much you can do about the porch, but during the day you can open the inside door and unfasten this glass panel on the storm door." He suited his words to action, and soon a nice breeze was cooling the house. "How about upstairs?"

"Oh, yes, please. If you have time," she added after a moment's hesitation, following closely behind when he went up the stairs. "This is the only room I use up here," she said as they approached the open door.

Lute's eyes swept her bedroom, and she was glad it was neat. Her robe, a gauzy cotton affair, was flung over the foot of the bed, but everything else was in order. A tightness gripped her throat at being with him here in her bedroom, where there was an unavoidable aura of intimacy surrounding them. Like one hypnotized, she watched him, and when he turned his eyes on hers, a startling thrill of desire coursed through her. Standing there, the sweat trickling down between her breasts, she felt more vulnerable than she ever had in her life. It was heart-stopping to see this handsome creature towering over her bed, and when his eyes dwelt an inordinate amount of time on her mouth, she could almost taste his lips on hers, feel his strong arms around her.

For what seemed an eternity they were held in suspended animation. Mesmerized, not daring to breathe, she drank him in with unquenchable eyes. Lute raised a hand—to touch her? she wondered fleetingly. She glimpsed the ring on his finger.

The spell was broken, reality returning like a kick in

the teeth. She turned quickly and went down the stairs.
The pain in her chest was almost more than she could bear,
but she was not going to crumple in front of him. Damned
if she would!

In the kitchen she bent over the sleeping dog, gently
stroking his satiny head and hoping her bleak hurt was
not visible in her eyes.

"He'll be all right," Lute said from behind her. "Mind
if I have a drink of water?"

Nelda stood quickly and moved to the sink. "I'm
sorry. I'll wash my hands and get some ice." She turned
on the tap, letting it run full force. The cold water on
her wrists and palms calmed her a little.

"The roast smells good. Do you want me to put it
back in the oven to keep it warm?"

Nelda dried her hands and took two glasses to the
refrigerator to fill with ice. "No. I'll probably eat it cold.
I'd invite you to share it, but I'm sure your wife is
expecting you home for dinner." They were the most
difficult words she'd ever had to say, and she tried fervently to keep her voice from betraying her desperation.
Before turning around, she said, "Cola or gingerale?"

When he didn't answer she turned, a glass of ice in
each hand. He was leaning against the counter, his eyes
on her face. She felt her pulse beating frantically at the
base of her throat. She stood waiting, leaving the refrigerator door open. He stepped forward, reached around
her, took out a large bottle of cola, and shut the door.
She moved to the cabinet and put the glasses down. He
came up behind her and, reaching around her again, set
the bottle on the counter.

"I've never had but one wife." His voice held a tenderness she didn't expect.

She swallowed hard and tried to control the trembling
of her chin. *Was he saying he wasn't married?* She
couldn't turn and face him; she was incapable of moving.

"But . . . the ring . . ." she whispered.

"I've worn it for eight years and five months. I can't get it off now."

A dam seemed to burst inside her. She could no more hold back the cry that tore from her throat than she could have stopped a steamroller. She bent over the counter, her face in her arms, her body convulsing as she began to sob. All the harrowing tension of the day—Kelly's accident, Lute's unnerving presence, and now the knowledge that he didn't belong to another woman after all—broke through all the barriers she'd been trying to erect. A torrent of tears came roaring from deep within her, and she cried, cried like a newborn, every vestige of self-control gone with the first sob.

Chapter

3

SHE KNEW LUTE'S eyes were on her back as grinding sobs wrenched her body. His arms reached for her, turned her around, and pulled her up against him. Cradling her head with one large hand, he wrapped his arms around her waist. Like a small child she nestled against him, her wet face pressed into the curve of his neck. The haven of his arms was a wonderful, safe cocoon, and minutes passed while he held her, crooned softly to her, and pushed back the riotous curls tumbling over her forehead. She felt him bury his face in her hair and stroke her trembling body from shoulder to behind, feeling each vertebra along her spine. She inhaled the lemony scent of his hair, tasted the salt of her own tears. It had been so long . . . so damn long. . . .

Her sobs subsided, reason returned, and Nelda tried to pull away, but the arms held her tightly. Embarrassment and shame for her loss of control almost started the tears again. She tried to turn her head so he couldn't see her blotchy, wet face, but it wasn't to be. He cupped her chin in his hand and tilted her face toward his.

"Oh, Lute! Please don't look at me. I'm so ashamed." She felt a tear escape over her lower lid and roll down her wet cheek. It must have been her imagination when she'd felt him bury his face in her hair.

"What happened? Is it Kelly? The doc said he was sure he'd be all right." His face was as concerned as his soft voice.

"I . . . don't know what got into me. It was just every-

33

thing coming all at once . . . and I . . . left the clothes on the line and a basket of wet ones . . . out there . . ." Her throat hurt with the effort to control her voice.

Lute laughed, and she felt it against her breast. "Is that all?" The deep voice was humoring her.

His face was close, so terribly close it was difficult to think what she was saying. His blue eyes, half shut, were within inches of her own, and his mouth, that firm-lipped mouth, was so near she could feel his breath on her lips. *Oh, God, I wish he'd kiss me!* The thought raced repeatedly through her mind. *Just once!* His lips opened, he seemed to hesitate, then he smiled.

"Go wash your face. You'd scare even Kelly if he woke up." There was a huskiness to his tone, and he dropped his arms and gave her a gentle push toward the bathroom. "When did you eat last?" his voice trailed her to the sink.

She was hurrying to wash her face, irrationally afraid he might vanish if she were gone too long. "This morning, I think. Cereal," she sputtered through the cold water.

"You think?" He was filling the glasses with soda when she came out of the bathroom. Her eyes clung to the ring on his finger . . . her ring . . . . He pushed a glass toward her, picked up his own and took a long swallow, poured in more cola, then returned the bottle to the refrigerator. "Drink your soda—it'll help to get some sugar into you. Then you can go hang up your wash. I'll make some gravy to go with that roast. I'm starving."

Nelda's heart lurched. Lute's face wavered in her vision. She felt precariously poised in a vacuum of weakness, lost in a fantasy that couldn't possibly be happening.

"Gravy?" she repeated incredulously. "I haven't had roast gravy since I left Iowa."

"Well, you're back, and you'll have some now. So get moving or I'll eat without you." It was the bossy, scolding tone he had used long ago when he'd said, "Come on. I'll not let you face your parents alone."

Nelda took a few sips of soda and hurried out the door before he changed his mind. The breeze cooled her hot face, and she lingered at the clothesline, taking down the dry sheets, folding them carefully, and then hanging the towels. Happiness played in her heart like a concerto, and she wanted it to last as long as possible.

She left the basket of dry linens on the porch and stood silently in the doorway watching Lute. She saw that he had lifted the meat onto a platter and placed a carving knife beside it. Now with sure, economical movements he was vigorously stirring the bubbling liquid in the roasting pan. She was admiring his efficiency— and the way his slim hips swiveled slightly as he mixed.

"I couldn't find the cornstarch, so I used flour," he said without turning around. She jumped, feeling every inch a spy at her own door, but he continued speaking conversationally as she entered the room. "Sometimes I get lumpy gravy with flour, never with cornstarch. Find me a tureen to put this into, stick some bread into the toaster, and set out the butter. I hate to spread hard butter."

"I remember," she said softly, more to herself than to him. Aloud she added, "I can make a salad."

"I don't think my stomach will wait for it. Why don't you just slice a few of those tomatoes?"

Nelda moved like a robot. She brought him the gravy boat, put the bread into the toaster, sliced the tomatoes, set the table, and then, remembering the butter, hurried to the refrigerator.

After looking to see that Kelly was sleeping comfortably, she sat across the table from Lute, still amazed that he was really there. His hair was damp and combed. He must have done that while she was at the clothesline. He pulled her plate toward him and arranged her dinner at the same time he fixed his own: a slice of buttered toast, then an abundant layer of sliced meat topped with a steaming ladle of gravy.

"Try that," he beamed. "That's a Hanson special."

Nelda laughed. It was really more of a giggle, and she realized she hadn't done that in years. "Looks good. Maybe you should open up your own place and run all the fast-food chains out of business."

"Not a bad idea," he said agreeably. He got up between forkfuls and slipped two more slices of bread into the toaster.

She wanted to know so much about him, but she was afraid to question him, afraid he would go all icy like he had at the cemetery.

"This is wonderful," she complimented honestly after taking a big bite. "I've never bought cornstarch. What else do you use it for beside making gravy?"

"Lots of things. White sauce, puddings, you name it."

"Well, thank you, Heloise! Where did you pick up all this valuable information?"

"4-H." He grinned brightly, and her heart did a rapid flip-flop. "I was a leader for a couple of years. Even the boys learn to cook these days, so I learned along with the boys and we picked up a few blue ribbons at the fair." The bread popped up and he stood to pluck it from the toaster. Holding one slice out to her, he offered, "More?"

"No, thanks. On second thought, yes, I believe I will," she responded, startled at her own appetite.

"Good. Hand me your plate and put more toast in for me. I've just gotten started."

The banter between them was light and nonstop. Both of them carefully kept the conversation on an impersonal footing. Nelda did pick up some fragments of information she tucked away in her mind to review more thoroughly later. He farmed, and there was a reference to a sale barn. Did he own it? Yes. Later he said *my* sale barn, which meant he did.

Finally she decided to risk a direct question. "Where do you live now, Lute?" She quaked inwardly; it was her first inquiry about his personal life.

"About two sections over." He jerked his head toward the back porch. "Didn't you know that that corn out there was mine? Well, not all mine. I guess it's part yours, too." He lifted questioning eyebrows. "I leased that land about four years ago. You didn't know that—even after your grandparents died?"

"No, I didn't know. Mr. Hutchinson said it was leased to Sweet Clover Farms, Incorporated, and I never asked who that was. It's really you?"

Lute smiled in an endearing way that lifted the corners of his mouth and spread a warm light into his eyes.

"Wouldn't your papa the banker be surprised to know that I didn't end up in the gutter after all?" Although he was smiling when he started to speak, by the time he finished, the warmth in his eyes was replaced by a steely cold gleam and his voice grated harshly.

Nelda hesitated. If she answered his jibe she would have to admit that, yes, her father would be surprised. She could remember with clarity her father's words regarding Lute: "Long-haired bastard! Why doesn't he get a haircut? Get a decent job? Wear socks, like respectable folks?"

"Dad was prejudiced against our generation, Lute. There's no doubt about that," she responded slowly.

Lute gave her a sharp glance and then lowered his eyes to his plate. The atmosphere was suddenly cooler. Her heart sank as she realized that he was putting *her* on trial, too. She hoped her stomach would settle down and that she wouldn't burst into tears again.

She pushed back her chair. "Would you like some coffee?"

"No, thank you. I've got to be going. Mom's putting

sweet corn in the freezer tomorrow, and I promised her I'd pick and husk it tonight."

"Your mother lives with you?"

"In the summer. I send her to the Rio Grande valley in the winter." He squatted beside Kelly and fondled the setter's ears. "He'll be out for a while yet. When he comes to he'll be thirsty, but don't let him fill up on water—it'll make him sick." He stood.

"Thanks for taking us to Gary's. I don't know how I'd have managed otherwise," Nelda said sincerely.

"You'd have managed," he responded in an inscrutable way. "Thanks for the supper. Or, I guess they say 'dinner' in New York." At the door he turned and looked at her.

She stood at the table, her hands clutching the rim of the ladder-backed oak chair.

"I saw your picture in a magazine after you'd decorated the club rooms in a fancy hotel. You looked like one of those jet setters. I never thought to see you here, living in a farmhouse, hanging clothes on the line. What are you trying to prove, Nelda?"

She felt as if he'd kicked her in the stomach. She could only stare, mesmerized. Inside, she was hollow, unable to think.

"Why should I be trying to prove something?" She heard her own voice dully echoing in a vacuum of despair. He thinks I must have an ulterior motive for coming here, she reflected. He wants to think I'll pack up and leave if the going gets rough. Mentally straightening her spine, she resolved that if it was proof he wanted, then proof he would get. If he wanted anything...

Lute lifted his shoulders as if he was no longer interested in the answer to his question. "I'll get my helmet out of your car," he said tersely as he left.

Nelda walked to the kitchen doorway and watched him. When he passed the steps he looked up at her. He lifted his arm briefly in salute, donned the helmet, and pulled the visor down. She watched him roll his motorcycle out into the lane, mount, and ride away. His departure took a little of the starch out of her determination, but she quickly reminded herself that it was every bit as important that she prove some things to *herself*.

As the days passed Nelda began to feel that at last she was the captain of her own fate. A sense of belonging settled over her, and she looked around the farmhouse with pride at what she had accomplished. The lawn was mowed, the flower beds dug, the garage cleaned out, and the Oldsmobile crowded into the building that was meant to house a Ford of the thirties. She'd had help from Ervin Olson with the small riding mower she'd found stored in the garage. She had been tinkering with it one morning when he pulled into the lane on one of his brief visits. When she'd asked him how to start the machine, he'd taken over the job of getting it into working condition. Hours later, in cut-off jeans and straw hat, Nelda was happily riding back and forth across the huge yard, and Ervin was grinning broadly. Climbing into his pickup, he'd announced he was off to spread the news: "Don't that beat all—old Severt's city granddaughter out mowing like an old hand. 'Course I'll have to take some of the credit myself," he chuckled merrily before tipping his hat and driving off.

The vet stopped by several times to check on Kelly. The big Irish setter was still stiff and sore and moved cautiously from the house to his favorite spot under the lilac bush. Nelda fretted and tried to cater to his every whim, constantly reminding herself of Gary's brisk announcement that in a few weeks Kelly would be "right as London rain."

"I think you've decided city life wasn't so bad after all, haven't you, fella?" Nelda said to him one day as she patiently held the screen door open so he could painfully climb the three steps necessary to reach the porch.

"Just as soon as you're able, we'll go for a long walk, and you'll begin to like it here again."

Gary's visits had certainly cheered many a morning or afternoon, Nelda had to admit to herself as she stooped to feed Kelly his chow. Now if only Lute would deign to brighten her doorway once in a while . . .

As if on cue, she heard the rumble of a pickup approaching the house. Ervin Olson had already made his "driveway visit," as Nelda had dubbed them, early that morning, and Gary had just left shortly before so it must be—could it be? Her heart hammered in anticipation.

Turning to the porch door again to greet her visitor, she caught a flash of gold as Lute's blond hair captured the sunlight when he swung down from the pickup and strode toward her.

"Hi there," she sang out cheerfully.

"How's the patient?" Lute grumbled, his blue eyes looking not at her but at the level of her knees, where he seemed to expect Kelly to materialize.

"Oh . . ." she said, trying not to let her disappointment find a voice, ". . . he just sat down to lunch." She tossed a dish towel over her forearm in the manner of the best New York sommeliers. "Now let's see, did he tell me the reservation was for one, or for two?" she mused. "Oh well, never mind, I'm sure we can find you an extra seat," she continued, warming to her rôle.

Lute stood looking at her, his expression a curious mix of amusement and exasperation.

"This way, sir," she concluded, hoping amusement would win out as she led the way through the kitchen door.

"Hey there, fella," came Lute's gruff voice from behind her. Kelly's ears pricked up, and he turned from his dish with a half wag of his tail. He limped over to Lute and nuzzled the hand that descended to pat his head, then he slowly circled around and returned to his chow.

"Well, his appetite's certainly none the worse for his injuries," Lute commented. "And he seems to be getting around. What does Gary have to say about him?"

When Lute didn't lift his gaze to her, for a moment Nelda found herself wishing she were an Irish setter—at least then she might get some attention from him.

"His prognosis is excellent—he expects Kelly to be back chasing motorcycles in just a few weeks," she informed him.

"Good."

He finally looked up at her, and over the sound of her galloping heart she said, "I meant what I said about lunch. Would you like to stay? Not on the floor, of course," she amended quickly, noticing his raised eyebrow.

"Thanks, but no. I've got to get back to work."

She listened for regret in his voice, but heard only what sounded like a subtle accusation. "Surely you can break for an hour or so to eat," she pressed.

"Maybe you're used to long lunches in New York, but here we're sometimes forced to skip the martinis and grab a sandwich while we work," he said tightly.

With his emphasis falling heavily on his last word, Nelda had no doubt that she'd interpreted the accusatory tone correctly. Miffed, all she could think of to fling at his retreating back was, "I don't even like martinis!" She thought she saw his broad shoulders shake with silent laughter before he pulled himself back into the cab.

The phone jangled, and Nelda stomped over to the counter to answer it. As she did so, she suddenly realized that she'd been living in the house for more than three weeks without receiving a local call. So far, most of her calls had been from New York: friends wondering when she was coming back to civilization, or decorating people picking up the loose ends of projects she'd worked on. She'd also had a call from her father in Florida. He'd made it plain he thought she had lost her mind to bury herself in north Iowa when she had a blossoming career going in New York.

This call was from Rhetta, the veterinarian's wife, and she wanted to know if it would be convenient for her to stop by that afternoon. Nelda was pleased she was going to have a real visitor. Though Ervin Olson and Gary often came by, they seldom stayed more than five minutes apiece, and she had to admit that she longed for a little chit-chat.

Right on time a four-wheel drive vehicle came up the lane and a tall, large-boned woman got out. She had thick wheat-colored hair tied at the nape of her neck, a suntanned face, and friendly brown eyes. Nelda met her at the back door.

"Hello. I'm Rhetta," the woman said, extending a hand in greeting.

"I'm Nelda, obviously. Do come in."

In ten minutes they were chatting as if they'd known each other for years.

"I tell you, Nelda, if I take on any more projects, Gary swears he's going to raffle me off at the next veterinary convention. I had decided I was simply *not* going to be the next president of the Women's Club even if they got down on their knees and begged me, and what did I do? I sat there like a fool and they elected me! Now I've got the membership drive, the charity ball, the drive to expand the library, etcetera, etcetera."

"Sounds as if you have your hands full. What about your children? Did you say they were twelve and fourteen?"

"Those boys are so self-sufficient they scare me! The only thing they'll ever need a woman for is sex. They cook, do their own laundry, clean their rooms, manage their own money. They both think the sun rises and sets with their father. Their other hero is Lute. He's taught them gun safety, how to drive a tractor—he even took them to the Minnesota north woods and taught them wilderness survival."

In order to hide her elation on hearing these things about Lute, Nelda got up and refilled their iced-tea glasses.

"Have you known Lute long?" she asked as casually as possible.

"Since we came here about six years ago. He's sure come a long way since then. At that time he was renting just a little place, but that boy worked like a son-of-a-gun! He bought that farm and another section to go with it. And I understand he leases another section. He's got equipment you wouldn't believe! Eighteen-row planters and all that. One of his tractor cabs is so plush it's even got stereo." Rhetta's large capable hands turned her glass around and around. Nelda sensed the woman's eyes glued to her while she talked about Lute.

Suddenly Nelda knew a question about her and Lute was coming, and before she could head it off it was asked.

"You *are* Nelda, the mother of Lute's little girl?"

"Yes," she said, and she was glad to admit it.

"I thought so. Nelda isn't a common name around here."

After a slightly awkward silence Nelda offered, "This was my grandparents' farm. It was left to me. The land is leased to Lute. I just found that out recently." She laughed nervously. "The farm manager said the land was leased to Sweet Clover Farms. It took me a while to think to ask who that was."

Nelda knew her eyes were bright and that her fingers were tightly gripping her glass. She also knew Rhetta noticed, and was thankful she was polite enough not to mention it.

"Yeah, our Lute's done well for himself," she said. "Did he tell you he owns the sale barn, too?"

"He did mention something about it."

"Well, I've got to scoot. I'm on the committee to raise

money for an indoor community swimming pool, and if
I don't want to be put in charge of one thing or another
I'd better be there to say no." She stood.

Nelda was surprised to realize how tall and sturdy her
new friend was. "Why a pool when you're so close to a
lovely lake?" she asked.

"The season is short here for one thing, and there are
so many cottages around the lake that it's beginning to
get dirty, and some years the fish die, and the
algae—"

"Stop, stop!" Nelda laughed. "I'm convinced."

"Good! I'll get you onto the committee."

"I'm not *that* convinced!" Nelda protested.

"Will you come to supper some night? It might be hot
dogs cooked on the grill. . . ."

"I love hot dogs," Nelda assured her.

"Ahhhhh . . ." Rhetta sighed with relief. "I thought
coming from New York you'd expect Chicken Kiev, or
something equally impossible for me to make."

"Just because I lived in New York is no sign I have
a gourmet appetite. I'm a lousy cook. Alongside one of
my meals, a TV dinner looks like a feast."

"That's comforting to hear. I hate people who do
everything well. Well, thanks for the tea and the chat.
Looks like it's going to storm. This hot sultry weather
could stir up a real doozy! We have a tornado alert system
in town, but I'm not sure you'd hear the sirens out here."
Rhetta talked nonstop until she slammed the car door.
Then she yelled, "'Bye," and shot off down the lane.

Nelda spent the rest of the afternoon going through a
box of pictures she'd found in a bureau. Grandma kept
everything, she mused. She sat on the bed in the small
room she'd used when she came to visit and carefully
scrutinized the faces in the pictures. Grandma and Grandpa
with a small boy who must have been her father between
them, a picture of him when he went away to school,
one with him and his first car, then him and her mother

standing beside the car. There were many pictures of
Nelda herself when she was little, too—in the swing,
with the chickens. . . . She stopped at a picture of her and
Lute standing beside his old pickup.

Nelda felt her throat swell. His hair wasn't as long as
she'd remembered—it hadn't even come down to his
shoulders. She had to laugh, remembering the beard he'd
tried to grow when they were in high school. He'd finally
gotten disgusted and shaved it off. And he'd been so
thin! But she'd been thinner then, too. Lute used to tease
her about her breasts. If they were any smaller, he used
to say, he'd have to find them with a magnifying glass.
And her hair looked awful! It was parted in the middle
and hung limply on each side of her face. The constant
straightening process had turned it to fuzz. Ugh!

Suddenly it was almost dark in the room, and she
heard the distant rumble of thunder. Leaving the pictures
scattered on the bed, she went downstairs and looked out
the back door. It was almost dark and the wind had picked
up. The clouds in the southwest were dark, rolling, and
split by streaks of lightning. Even Kelly seemed to realize
this was not the usual rainstorm. He stood close beside
her and pressed his nose to the screen.

"It'll be all right, boy. It's going to rain, that's all.
You stay here while I run out and shut the garage window
and close the doors."

She squeezed in between the car and the wall and
closed the small window over the tool bench, then tugged
at the double swinging doors, finally getting them closed
and the clasp fastened.

As she neared the house she heard the telephone ring,
and she ran the rest of the way. By the time she reached
the porch the ringing had stopped. Just as well, she
thought, I'm in no mood to talk about color and fabric
today.

She went through the house lowering the windows on
the south and west. She wasn't frightened until she re-

turned to the porch and saw that the darkness had triggered the mechanism that turned on the yard light, and it was only six o'clock.

The wind hit the house with a sudden blast. Nelda saw a tree branch snap, fall onto the garage, and slide down the peaked roof to the ground. She didn't know what she should do, but she was sure she shouldn't be standing on a glassed in porch.

When the black pickup truck came careening up the lane and slammed to a stop beside the porch, Nelda stood quietly waiting. The wonderment that Lute was here gripped her, and all fear of the storm disappeared.

The door was almost torn from his hand when he opened it to get into the house. The wind had blown his hair into disarray, and his shirt was plastered to his body by the heavy raindrops that had already started falling.

"Why the hell didn't you answer the phone?" he barked when he finally got the door closed and fastened. "Why aren't you in the basement? Didn't you have the radio on, or hear the sirens?"

"No. I—"

He grabbed her hand. "Oh, for heaven's sake! A funnel was sighted a few miles from here, headed this way." He dragged her to the door leading to the basement and flung it open. "Get down there. Do you have a battery-powered radio?"

"Yes. In my bedroom."

"I'll get it. Now get down those steps, and take the dog with you."

She switched on the light and went part way down the steep wooden stairs, Kelly close beside her. She didn't like being in the basement—it was full of cobwebs and spiders.

Suddenly the wind stopped blowing, and it was deadly quiet except for the sound of Lute's boots tromping down the stairs, hurrying across the kitchen and down the basement steps. He pushed Nelda into the corner of the basement and stood over her. He pressed his body against hers, and she automatically wrapped her arms about his waist.

"Lute, what is it?"

"Shhhh . . . listen."

Out of the silence they heard it coming. On it came, roaring like a hundred freight trains. The noise grew so intense that it seemed to merge with her very being, and she clutched at Lute's shirt.

"Lute!"

He wrapped his arms around her, and they sank to the floor. "Don't be afraid. This is the best place to be." On his knees he pulled her between his legs, his thighs gripped her hips, his hand cupped the back of her head, his arms and shoulders shielded her. She was surrounded by him.

With her body fitted into his like a hand in a glove, her senses refused to think about anything but the feel of him, the smell that was totally male with overtones of lime soap and aftershave. His cheek was pressed tightly to hers, and she could feel the flexing of the muscle in his jaw. She wanted desperately to turn her face and feel the touch of his lips, but he held her head in a viselike grip. She opened her mouth against his neck. The heaven of it! It was pure heaven to feel and taste him. Lute . . . her only love.

The roar of the wind lasted for several minutes, and then it was gone. Lute raised his head. The weak cellar lights had gone out, but the floor of the kitchen was still over them.

"Is it over?" Nelda whispered the question, her nose pressed tightly to his neck.

"I think so, but we'll wait a minute to be sure."

He turned his face, and she could feel the soft, silky brush of his mustache, then his mouth, against her cheek. It was more than she could bear. She wrenched her mouth from his neck and blindly, desperately, sought the warm comfort of his. Her mouth blended into his with such force it seemed to rock the world. Their instinctive, undeniable need for each other was a force suddenly unmitigated by reason. They clung to each other as if compelled by fear that the naked hunger they sought to appease would be unfulfilled.

Nelda's arms clutched him to her in agony over thoughts that he might pull away. But the arms that gripped her, and the hand that moved to cup her firm bottom and press her against what deemed him man, was an unmistakable indicator that his desire was as strong as hers. Desperate with hunger, they deepened the kiss. It was a merging, as if his mouth was her mouth and hers was his, lips, tongues, teeth, all one.

Lute's chest was heaving, he was breathing hard. He withdrew his mouth, dragging it a fraction from hers so she could breathe. Seemingly reluctant to leave, his lips and tongue stayed at the corner of her mouth while his nose pressed into her soft cheek.

"Oh, God. Oh, God!" The words came out of his throat in a growl of agony. He was trembling violently and holding her so tightly she could feel every bone, every pulse, every corded muscle. She couldn't bear for it to end here.

"Please . . ." It was a whispered plea, and she wasn't sure he heard it.

The firm mouth fastened on hers again, molding it, sculpting the soft flesh, breathing life into it. The meeting of tongues was like a homecoming. The fierce possession lasted several minutes, then gradually the kiss was tempered by gentleness as if the explosion of their first coming together was subsiding into an aftermath of the exquisite wonder of rediscovery. He nibbled at her lips with his, stroked them with his tongue, pulled her lower lip into his mouth. Small sounds came from her throat and were lost in his. His hand roamed her back, soothing, caressing, then wandering and burrowing beneath her shirt to find her soft, unrestrained breasts that were flattened against his chest.

The world had stopped. There was only this holding, touching, tasting, of each other—until Kelly growled.

Slowly Lute lifted his head. Nelda refused to open her eyes, wanting to stay here forever. Gripping her arms, he moved her away from him. He got slowly to his feet. Nelda's muscles, cramped from kneeling, were slow to respond to the command to move. He pulled her up beside him and leaned her against him until the blood could circulate to her legs.

"I'm so glad you were here," she whispered, but he didn't answer.

Chapter

4

HE HAD HEARD the soft words.

"So am I." He paused, then added, "Or you might have been blown away."

The basement was so dark she couldn't see his face, but the breath that fanned hers told her it was near. She couldn't stop trembling. She knew the chill that shook her was only partly due to the cold and the dampness of Lute's shirt that had seeped into her own.

Kelly growled again. He was leaning heavily against her legs. This was the first time he had been in the basement—she had never been able to coax him down before. Now he wanted out.

They felt their way up the steps, and Lute opened the kitchen door. It was lighter in the kitchen, and she could see dim outlines. They made their way to the porch. The rain was still coming down in sheets, but during the intermittent flashes of lightning they could see the havoc the storm had created. The roof of the garage was gone, and the sides leaned crazily against the Oldsmobile. A large branch had split from the elm tree, and it lay splintered across the bed of Lute's truck. The empty corn crib and the brick silo still stood, and the barn seemed to have survived intact.

"I didn't realize . . . I'd forgotten how destructive the wind can be." Nelda was appalled at the damage.

"That was no ordinary wind. That was a tornado. A town south of here was almost blown away a couple years ago. I knew what it could do."

"Oh, Lute! Thank you for coming. . . ." She took hold of his arm and looked into his face.

He moved away and went back to the kitchen. "The phone's out, too," he said from the gloom. "I've got to find out if Mom's all right."

"You're leaving?" she gasped in sudden desperation.

"No. I've got a C.B. in the truck. I'll go out and give a call."

She opened her mouth to ask if he couldn't wait until it stopped raining, but he was already out the door. She watched him run to the truck, then stood there immobilized, her eyes riveted to him. When the lightning flashed she could see the outline of him sitting in the truck. It seemed to her that her heart had stopped beating. Her world, her reason for existing, was hanging in limbo until he was back with her.

It was really Lute out there, she thought incredulously. The boy who had kissed her so awkwardly at first, until they learned together the joy of soft, tender, merging kisses, the boy who had trembled so violently when his fingers found their way into her blouse . . . and she didn't push him away. Her love! Together they had made a child, and somehow in the confusion of her own immaturity, her parents' intervention, and Lute's desire to be his own man, she had focused all her attention on Becky—and then herself—unthinking, not realizing *his* need.

"Lute . . . darling . . ." she whispered, "I can make it up to you. I know I can."

His clothes were soaking wet when he returned. He stood dripping on the floor, for once looking undecided about what to do.

"Was your mother all right?" Nelda asked softly, afraid the sound of her voice would send him back out into the rain.

"She was fine, and there was no damage done except to the crops. Cornstalks are all over the place, so the funnel must have touched down in the field and then bounced up and over my house and yours."

"I'll get some towels so you can dry off." She felt as if her heart would gallop right out of her breast. He had slipped out of his muddy boots and set them on the mat beside the door when she returned with the towels. She watched him rub the towel vigorously over his blond head, then peel off the wet shirt and drop it beside his boots. In the gloom his shoulders, chest, and flat stomach appeared to be the same color as his tanned face.

"I'd put your shirt in the dryer, but no electricity," she commented feebly. Her eyes clung to him. He was rubbing the towel over his shoulders and chest.

"My jeans are wet, too." His voice came out of the near darkness, and Nelda wished fervently for another flash of lightning so she could see him.

He spoke abruptly, without ceremony. "Do you want me to take them off, Nelda?"

Had he said what she thought he'd said? Oh, God, it was going to be up to her to decide! Could she be brazen enough to do it? Did she want him to make love to her— that was what he was asking....

"You could catch cold if you don't," she said in a breathless whisper, then she spun around and left the kitchen. At the newel post at the foot of the stairway she stopped and locked her hands about the rounded top. Her face burned, and her stomach muscles clenched and unclenched. Her breathing and heartbeat were all mixed up, as if their normal rhythm had gone awry and she couldn't get it back. It seemed to her that she stood there for an eternity. Then he was there, behind her.

Large, warm hands came up under her shirt, circled her ribcage, and pulled her back against his chest. His face found the curve of her neck, lips nibbled, his mustache tantalized her skin. She turned in his arms and wrapped hers around his naked torso. The need for him blazed crazily in her brain. It was dangerous to give herself as she was giving now; she was probably asking for rejection later. She pushed the thought from her mind. She wouldn't think of pain, humiliation...not tonight.

Arms around each other, they climbed slowly up the stairs.

At the door of her bedroom she turned and pressed herself against him, her arms locking themselves about his waist.

"Tell me we're not crazy, Lute," she whispered urgently against a pulse throbbing at the side of his neck.

"I can't...because we are!" he rasped. "But don't tell me to go!"

She loosened herself from his arms, and in one quick motion she whisked her knit shirt up over her head. It was her answer. Their arms reached for each other. He crushed her to him, flattening her breasts against his chest. Hungry mouths searched, found each other, and held with fierce possession. She gloried in the feel of him. Her hands couldn't stop caressing the smooth skin of his back—up and down they moved, and into the waistband of his shorts. She caressed his hips, which were taut, making deep hollows in the sides as the driving force of his desire strained to meet hers.

He broke away gasping. Urgent hands found the snap on her jeans, fumbled with the zipper, pushed them down. She stepped out of them at the same time she slipped her feet from her sandals.

The next moment they were flat on the bed. His naked body covered hers and he rained fervent kisses on her face.

"Nelda...my Nelda," he whispered hoarsely.

A deep longing compelled her to meet his passion equally. She kept her eyes tightly shut, not wanting to come out of the dreamlike state she was in. But suddenly she was wildly, burningly awake, and the driving force of her feeling was taking her beyond herself into a mindless void where there were only Lute's lips, Lute's hands,

Lute's hard, demanding body.

Without hesitation their bodies joined in mutual, frantic need. She heard sounds of his smothered groans, as if they came from a long way to reach her ears. Incredibly their pleasure rose to almost intolerable heights as soon as he entered and filled her. As they merged in a long, long unbelievable release she was aware of nothing but spiraling heights and the broad shoulders she clung to so she wouldn't slip off the edge of the world.

After a long moment, Lute supported himself on his elbows and gazed into her face.

"So quick . . . but I knew you were ready." He brushed the hair back from her face with a gentle hand.

She lay her palms against his cheeks, her thumbs caressing his lips and the silky hair above them. "I like it," she murmured, stroking the mustache before she pulled his head down to trace his lips with the tip of her tongue. She could feel his body demanding more, now that initial frustration had been appeased.

His beloved weight pressed her gently but securely to the bed. His heart was pounding against her breast, and it surprised her that she could even feel it over the hammering of her own. With a groan she could hear reverberating in his chest, he drew her tongue into his mouth and then searched the depths of hers in a gentle, sensuous exploration.

His hands found her small, rounded breasts. The feel of his rough palms stroking her nipples touched invisible strings that carried a fiery message to the depth of her femininity. He was quivering with the effort to love her leisurely, but tenderness was not what she needed. She ached for a surging rhythm with him, and her hips began to move. Still he dallied, moving his head down her body until his mouth was at her breast, and his tongue, rough and wet, sent another fiery summons. When she felt certain she would explode with longing, he was there, firm and wonderful as before. Then she did explode —

within. As soon as the first fantastic sensation died away, there was another, and then he began to thrust with unbelievable force again and again, until he arched his back with an inarticulate cry and they slipped into uncharted but beautiful oblivion.

Seemingly awed into silence by what had happened between them, Lute slid to her side and gathered her gently to him, cradling her head on his chest. He ran his rough palm over her nipple and she flinched not unpleasantly at its tenderness.

"I didn't intend to be so rough, Nelda," he whispered seriously. "I was so hungry for you I couldn't help myself." He moved his hand down her side, patted her bare bottom affectionately, and lifted her leg so that it rested across his thighs.

Nelda turned her lips to the smooth skin of his shoulder. They had separated from each other long enough to get properly into the bed and cover their naked bodies with a sheet. The rain that stayed behind when the storm moved out pounded against the roof. More content, happier than she could remember being, she lay molded to his side, her arm across his hard, flat stomach, his hand caressing her arm. Her fingers sought the hard nipples on his smooth chest, and a giggle escaped her.

"What brought that on?" Lute's hand moved to cup her rounded bottom.

"I was thinking about the three hairs you had on your chest. Remember? We'd gone to the state park on a picnic and were lying on a blanket when I discovered them."

"I remember," he said gruffly. "You pulled one of them out!" he accused.

She was elated that he had remembered, and her laugh was soft and happy.

"And I lost it on the blanket. I wanted to take it home."

"And I wanted to kiss you, but we had to look for that damn hair."

"We didn't find it, and you ran out into the water so

I couldn't get another one."

"I only had two left!"

"Oh . . . Lute. . . ." A little whimper escaped her lips.

"You can't turn back the clock, Nelda. That was a happy time of our life, but it ended in pain. I wouldn't like to relive it."

The tone of his voice ravaged her, sending a shiver of dread down her spine. She turned her face into the hollow of his shoulder, her fingers on his chest still. "I know," she murmured.

They fell into a warm, languid silence not unlike the peace of that summer day at the beach so long ago. Lute's hands continued to stroke her body gently, his breathing slower, his heart beneath her palm quieter. The feeling of panic and tension was gone. She pushed aside thoughts of morning, blocking out everything but this moment, this night.

He stirred, and his lips touched her forehead.

"What are you thinking?" she asked, tilting her head so she could rub her nose against his chin.

"This. . . . " The hand that hugged her buttocks pulled her tightly to his hip bone.

"Well . . ." she teased.

"I could have you again. You're a great temptation."

"Well . . ." Her fingers walked up his chest to his cheek and held it while she nibbled at his mustache. *"Now* what are you thinking?" she murmured when he lay motionless.

"We didn't take any precautions, unless you . . ."

A chill went over her. "You mean unless I'm on the pill? What the hell do you think I am?" Anger and hurt made her voice raspy. "You think I take the pill every day in hopes someone will come by and I can have a tumble in bed? Is that what you think of me, Lute?" She knew she was being unreasonable, but she couldn't help it. She tried to pull away from him, but his arms tightened.

"That isn't what I think, and you know it." His arms bound her to him, not letting her move even a hairs-breadth away. "But how long has it been for you, Nelda?" The words seemed torn out of him. "How long? Don't try to tell me bed-hopping isn't an accepted thing with the crowd you've been in."

"No, I won't try to tell you that," she whispered, trying to staunch her pain. "I did try it briefly, Lute, and I hated it! It was so . . . cold, so mechanical. Please don't spoil this. Don't put it on that level," she pleaded.

His heart was beating heavily again under the palm that still lay on his chest. His silence was unsettling, and she stared into the darkness, taut with a feeling of hu-miliation and helplessness. She knew he was judging her again, and her defensiveness made her angry.

"I didn't mean that." The words rasped from his throat.

"Then what the hell did you mean?" Her voice trem-bled with irrational agony. "I'm surprised you don't carry something with you like you used to do . . . after it was too late!"

"Stop it!" His mouth searched for hers in a fierce, possessive motion to silence it, forcing it to open beneath his own. She moaned and fought the invasion of her mouth and tried to push him away. His arms held her in a viselike grip, and his naked legs held hers imprisoned. She struggled. *None of this means any more to him than any other diversion for the night. He's not feeling or remembering any of the things I'm feeling.* . . . Her eyes were tightly closed, though tears pricked beneath the lids. Suddenly her mouth was free.

"Oh, Nelda Elaine, you haven't changed a bit." His laugh was low and tender, and his lips covered her face with gentle kisses. "You still get carried away by your emotions."

Total confusion swamped her mind. "You know I hate to be called that," she pouted, embarrassed by her child-ishness but childishly happy at his dubious endearment.

"I remember." His lips, firm yet gentle, sought hers. In his earlier effort to hold her he had rolled her onto her back and pinned her with the length of his body. Her arms now slid about his neck and she tugged gently on the hair on the back of his head. He began to kiss her deeply, his touch sensuous and languid, taking his time, exploring her slowly, setting her ablaze with hunger, making her give herself up to him. Her breath came fast and light, his thick and gasping.

She moved her legs to encompass his when his lips descended to the warm curve of her throat and the rounded flesh of her breast. His mouth slid gently over her sensitized skin until it enclosed her nipple and fondled the stiff peak.

A current of pleasure mixed with fear washed over her as his lips moved back up her body, searching for her mouth in the darkness, finding it, and melding her lips to his. *He has the power to make me mindless in his hands!* After the first deep pressure of his mouth, he lifted it and leisurely, tenderly, almost reverently, made love to her mouth with warm, soft lips and exploring tongue. He kissed, nibbled, licked, caressed until she was conscious of nothing but his touch.

Her breath came in small gasps when his mouth would allow it, and small volcanoes of sensation erupted within her, sending her blood, suffused with molten fire, flooding riotously through her body. Suddenly she didn't care that there were no precautions being used, and she trembled and twisted beneath him, trying to make him realize that nothing mattered except satisfying their desperate need for each other.

They swirled in a mindless vortex of pleasure created by caressing fingertips, clinging mouths, biting teeth, and closely entwined limbs. She kissed his face, his neck, his shoulder, and clutched at his buttocks to keep his throbbing warmth inside her. He began to move gently at first, and her nerves responded like fine, taut strings under the bow of a master violinist. She clung to him, aware only of the rhythmic gliding that was pushing her higher and higher toward a bursting, shivering note that was beyond the range of any ears except Lute's and hers. The crescendo was long and rapturous, forceful but ecstatic, and the lingering strains only more endearing than the other times.

Time and again during the night he drew her to him, seemingly tireless, murmuring softly of the hunger that gnawed at him and the thirst for the mouth she offered so willingly. Exhaustion finally sent him into a deep sleep and Nelda into that limbo between unconsciousness and awareness. She lay molded to his body, her cheek nestled in the warm hollow of his shoulder. She loved him and wanted to be with him forever, and she wondered longingly if that could ever be. Surely he'd heard the blessed music of their lovemaking.

As she lay quietly beside him, he turned and buried his face in the curve of her neck, like a child seeking comfort. She held him and stroked the hair back from his forehead, loving him, wanting him to love her in return. But she couldn't dismiss a feeling of impending doom. Her need for him was making her a prisoner! In torment she tightened her arms around him and pressed her mouth to his cheek, and finally fell asleep wishing he would embrace her in return.

Morning came too quickly.

Nelda instantly wakened to full awareness. She was cuddled in Lute's arms, her bare legs entwined with his. Suddenly he stiffened and, wrenching himself away from her, sat up in bed.

"What is it? What's wrong, Lute?"

"It's daylight. I've got to go." He swung his legs off the bed.

"Your clothes are probably still damp. I'll put them in the dryer if the electricity is on." His naked back and buttocks were toward her, and the ecstasy she had shared with him came rushing back.

"Don't bother," he responded tersely. He was pulling on the shorts he had abandoned so hastily the night before. "I must have been out of my mind!" he rasped. His eyes were cold, ruthless, and glittering strangely as they roamed over her face.

The shock of seeing him in this mood was like a dash of cold water after a warm bath.

At the door he looked back at her with narrowed eyes, and he spoke in a sharp, cruel voice.

"I don't need you in my life, Nelda. You don't fit into my life-style now any more than you ever did. I'm a farmer, remember? I'll always have dirt under my nails."

Nelda lay still, unable to move or utter a sound. Shaken to the core, she tried to think of something to say in her defense . . . but what was she defending?

"I didn't drag you in here, Lute." Her voice was surprisingly calm.

His laugh was sudden and seemed to owe little to humor. "That's true. But what'd you expect if you put a stallion in a stall with a mare in heat?"

She gasped but didn't allow him to see that his crudeness cut into her heart like a knife.

"That's unworthy of you, Lute," she said quietly.

He glared at her for a moment and was gone.

When the echoes of the back door slamming died away, Nelda's first reaction was that of relief. He was gone, she was alone, she could let down her guard and cry if she chose. But she didn't cry.

"You really asked for it, didn't you, you poor, dumb broad." It was weird to be talking to herself this way, to feel as if she didn't belong to herself, but somehow she needed sound. "All this time it was in the back of your stupid little mind to see Lute and try to win him back, and you know it!" She wanted to laugh, but laughter wouldn't come. Depression did. It settled over her like a shroud. She felt lonely, lost, and then frantic. She

began to shiver. The look in Lute's eyes when he walked
away would stay in her mind forever. She wanted to hate
him, but all she could hate was her own weakness for
him. She sat up in bed so fast her head began to whirl
dizzily.

Kelly stood in the doorway, his tail swishing happily.
He bounded into the room and then back to the door
expectantly. His obvious need to go out moved Nelda to
get up, slip into her robe, and follow him down the stairs.

She stood at the back door and looked at the storm
damage with dulled eyes. One wall of the garage leaned
on the Oldsmobile. Branches and parts of the garage roof
were scattered over the yard. Lute's truck, the huge tree
limb sprawled across its bed, still stood beside the well
house. He must have walked home, she thought numbly.

At least the phone was working again. Nelda drank
a whole pot of coffee and took a bath before she called
Mr. Hutchinson, the farm manager. He assured her he
would have someone out to clear away the debris and
assess the damage done to her car. Did she need transportation while her car was being repaired? She told him
she did, and he offered to arrange a rental. He asked if
she wanted the garage rebuilt, and if she did, he assumed
she would want it attached to the house for convenience.
Nelda replied without hesitation that she did indeed want
it replaced—but on the old foundation and in the same
style as before. Didn't he know adding a modern garage
to the eighty-year-old farmhouse would totally destroy
its charm?

She hung up the phone, wondering why his casual
assumption had made her so angry.

Chapter

5

LATE THE NEXT morning Nelda heard the buzz of a motorcycle approaching. Her heartbeat skipped to double-time, and her hands froze to the edge of her workbench. As the roar got louder she stood to reassure Kelly, who quickly scuttled away from where he'd been resting at her feet and hurried through the open door into the kitchen. She didn't know whether to be happy or sad at his new cautiousness, but soon her attention was inexorably drawn to the cycle itself now roaring into the lane. She watched its approach through the porch windows, nervously recalling Lute's conjecture that he was the only motorcyclist in the area.

She'd known he would have to return for his truck, and she had mentally steeled herself for his visit. As planned, she decided to return to her workbench and assume a studied indifference. After several minutes of staring blankly at its surface, however, she heard a different kind of buzzing. Her curiosity getting the better of her, she edged back to the window. Sure enough, it was Lute—there was no mistaking those powerful arms wielding the small power saw over the tree limb on his truck bed. Wanting nothing more than to dash out the door and throw herself into his strong embrace, she nonetheless realized that to do so would be as dangerous emotionally as it was physically. What was left of her pride would be cut to ribbons as readily as the huge limb was being dismembered.

With a heavy heart she moved into the house, closing

the door behind her and wishing that her longing could be muffled as easily as the whine of the saw. She puttered about aimlessly until there was silence. Waiting for the roar of the motorcycle—or would he now take the truck?—she instead heard a tapping at the back door.

What could he want? What could he possibly have to say? Her thoughts hopped about inside her head like so many penned rabbits. Her question was answered sooner than she thought when she opened the door.

"Where would you like the wood stacked?"

"Wood?" she responded blankly, wondering if her head were suddenly made of it.

"The fallen limb. I've cut it into firewood lengths. I'd stack it by the garage, but there isn't much left of a garage just now. Do you want it here by the porch steps?"

"Uh, yes, that'd be just fine. Thank you, Lute," she replied, trying to recapture a remnant of her "studied indifference."

He turned and trotted down the steps, heading back toward the truck. She watched the sun dance on his blond hair as he bent and straightened, his strong back and long strides making quick work of carrying and stacking the wood.

As he carried the last bundle toward the porch, she opened the door and walked onto the top step. "Would you like some iced tea?" she offered in what she hoped was not a squeaky voice.

He straightened up from depositing the last bundle, a deep breath puffing his broad chest. He looked to Nelda like a sunbronzed patron saint of clean, hard work, and once again she was held captive in his masculine aura.

He appeared to hesitate, then tossed out a dry, "No thanks. I'd best be getting back to work."

She heard the accusation in his voice, and it almost made her lash out at him. Forcibly restraining herself, she said simply, "Are you sure you won't change your mind?" He seemed to consider her for a moment. "That was quite a job you did," she explained weakly.

Throwing his shoulders back, he shook his head and started to turn away. He paused and asked, "Will you be getting some transportation?"

Inordinately pleased at even this minor show of concern, Nelda bubbled, "Yes. Mr. Hutchinson said he'd have a car delivered and—"

"Good," he interrupted brusquely. "I know you wouldn't want to be stranded out here indefinitely." He strode to his bike, calling over his shoulder that he'd be back for his truck later. The day for Nelda was suddenly bleak, despite the bright sun and cloudless sky.

The telephone rang, and she retreated slowly into the house to answer it. It was Rhetta again—her calls always seemed to follow Lute's departure, Nelda mused—calling to see how she had fared during the storm and to invite her to dinner the following weekend.

"I'd love to come." Nelda had to force the eager tone into her voice.

"There'll be eight of us plus the boys. Don't dress up, for heaven's sake! We'll probably cook something on the grill. In another few weeks it'll be too cold to cook outside. Oh, yes...one of our friends is building a house on the lakeshore. He could hardly contain himself when I told him we had a real live decorator from New York in our midst. He'll be at the party, so you just may find yourself with a job."

"Oh, Rhetta, I don't think I want to take on anything like that. I specialize in decorating commercial properties. You know, offices, cocktail lounges, stores. I—"

"That's okay, that's okay. He lives in Des Moines in the winter, and sometimes Minneapolis..." Rhetta talked on and Nelda half listened. "We're dying to get you onto the committee. We need some new blood," Rhetta's voice broke into her self-absorption.

"Don't plan on me, Rhetta. I may not be here that

long. I...have pressures to return to New York. I've still not decided yet."

"Oh, no!" Rhetta wailed. "Promise you'll give us a chance to grow on you. We're really quite nice people out here. Gary got used to us after living in London all his life."

"I'll certainly be here until Saturday night anyway," Nelda laughed. "I'll see you then."

When she hung up the phone she sat beside it for a long moment. It had been nice talking to Rhetta. Maybe she needed more women friends, she mused. She'd never been one to have close girl friends. From the time she was sixteen she'd had Lute. Although they didn't go to the same school, they had spent all their spare time together, much to the chagrin of her parents.

Lute! Nearly everywhere her thoughts wandered, he was there. How had she managed to carry on all those years in New York, she wondered. New York—that was how she had managed it. She'd been far enough away— and totally occupied in something that had no relationship to Lute. Maybe she *should* sell the farm, go away and never return. She doubted she could ever purge her thoughts of him now, after...

She pulled herself up short and concluded that at least somewhere else there wouldn't be as many reminders. But what had become of the Nelda who was resolved to provide proof of her maturity, her talent, her stamina— to Lute, to herself? Damn! How was she ever going to straighten out her life?

Thankfully her inner struggles were called to a halt right after a light lunch of some cockeyed tuna salad she'd thrown together while jousting with her mental giants. A crew of men arrived to take the sides of the garage down so her car could be removed. Looking as battle-scarred as Nelda felt, it was towed away behind a wrecker. After the yard had been cleared and the debris piled for hauling away, a bright red pickup truck was parked behind the house. A man brought the keys to the door and told her it would take several weeks to repair the body of her Oldsmobile, as some of the parts would have to be ordered.

Once the men left, the light slowly dawned on Nelda. A pickup truck! They'd brought her a pickup truck! What in hell was she supposed to do with that? A call to Mr. Hutchinson confirmed that it was all the rental agency had available. Ervin Olson popped into her mind, and automatically she found herself mouthing his all-encompassing expression of surprise, doubt, awe, or disbelief. "Now don't that beat all," she muttered, finally able to chuckle wryly at herself. "Well, Nelda girl, it's on from mental ogres to mechnical ones, I guess."

Not having any urgent errands to run, she decided to postpone tackling the pickup for a while. She puttered about the farmhouse for two days, occasionally cursing out the window or over the clothesline at the pickup. She continued working on her block prints, but the creative juices refused to flow—nothing looked right. The pattern she had chosen for her first print suddenly seemed all wrong, and she couldn't understand why—a few days before she'd thought it perfect.

Occasionally she stood on the porch and watched the new garage take shape. One morning when she did so she noticed that Lute's truck was gone. He must have come awfully early—to avoid seeing her? she wondered. She had to admit that much of the joy had gone out of living in the farmhouse. She seriously considered packing her personal things, driving to Minneapolis, and taking a plane east. Poor Kelly. He'd have to be sedated before they could get him into a flight cage; he'd been terrified during the one trip he'd taken. She patted his head in retroactive sympathy. Oh well, he'd just have to endure.

Nelda would almost talk herself into going, and the next minute she would declare, "Hell, no! I haven't done what I came here to do. And I'm no nearer making a decision on whether or not to sell the farm than I was when I got here. Oh, Lute! Damn you! Get out of my mind . . . get out of my heart, you . . . bastard!"

On the third day she relented toward her nearest scapegoat, the red pickup parked in the drive, and decided it was about time she tried driving it. Who knew when there might be an emergency and she'd have to use it? And in the meantime, she was getting low on groceries and dog food. "Nothing ventured, nothing gained," she muttered to Kelly. "So come on, fella, let's see if we can't start 'er up."

Trotting out with Kelly at her heels, she didn't even have to unlock the truck door before she spotted the stick shift. It just figured, particularly since she hadn't driven a standard since she was a teenager. With some trepidation she climbed into the driver's seat—and found her feet dangling helplessly, inches from the pedals. Groaning, she pulled the seat forward as far as she could, and even then she had only a precarious toe-hold on the clutch. Wracking her memory for the proper starting procedure, she slid foward to depress the clutch, turned the ignition key, and heard a satisfying surge as the powerful engine jumped to life. Excitedly she urged the shift into what she hoped was first gear, yelling "Wish me luck" to a bemused Kelly, who lay watching from the grass below. At that moment her toes slid from the clutch and the truck bucked to a protesting stall. Stunned but not daunted, she returned the shift to neutral and repeated her tactic, sitting as close to the wheel as possible to get a better grip on the deep clutch. This time, depressing the accelerator more enthusiastically to insure her start, she tried to gently release the clutch pedal. The truck immediately lurched backward, bouncing her against the wheel and back again, and predictably ground to a stall as her feet again left the pedals. Damn! She'd had it in reverse! Almost wailing in frustration, she gingerly began the routine again. Perspiring nervously and cursing in a decidedly unladylike way, she tried several more times, but to no avail. Feeling thoroughly insulted by this indirect attack on her capabilities, she thrust the pedals down, threw the ignition—and nothing happened. Now what! Fuming and fiddling with the key, she could get no more than a healthy purr from the battery.

The sound of a pickup pulling into the lane caught her attention, and she could hardly decide whether she was relieved or embarrassed that Ervin Olson had chosen this moment for one of his driveway visits. She was stunned when a strong hand clasped her elbow as she stepped down from the cab backwards.

She slowly turned and looked up into Lute's laughing eyes. What was *he* doing here?

Answering her silent question, he chuckled. "Looks like I got here just in time. I thought maybe if your car hadn't arrived, you might be needing help...." He paused, "...or some dog food for Kelly."

"Well, you were right about the dog food, but wrong about my needing help," she snapped. "I was just heading for the market when...I realized I hadn't brought my purse," she fabricated quickly.

He gazed at her from head to toe, taking in her be-draggled appearance and, she knew, not missing the small detail of her bare feet.

"We may be rural, Nelda, but most folks around here wear shoes when they go shopping," he enunciated slowly, barely concealed laughter evident in his tone. "I thought maybe it was a problem with the truck. Sounded to me like you flooded it."

"Is that what I did?" she said, immediately realizing she'd admitted her plight.

"Here, let me help you," he offered more gently. "The seat's too far back for a little lady," he added, his emphasis falling on his last words.

She recalled her rumpled appearance and winced. He said no more, and she watched as his greater strength allowed him to easily slide the ornery seat into a more accessible position for her. Grudgingly she thanked him.

"Can I offer you some iced tea?"

He glanced into her eyes, and she knew they both remembered that this was her third invitation.

"I thought you were going shopping," he ventured. "I wouldn't want to hold you up. Besides, I'd best get back to work." This time when he said it she didn't notice any hostility in his voice, but she bristled nonetheless.

"That's right, I do have to go shopping, but I would have given you something to drink if you weren't so busy," she said in her defense. "So thank you for your help."

He nodded, turned, and ambled back to his own truck. "Sorry you obviously couldn't get a car on such short notice. Good luck with the truck," he offered in parting.

She watched his retreating back, and grudgingly admired his broad shoulders and tapering hips as he climbed into his truck, waved, and drove off.

"Damn trucks, damn men—damn Lute!" she muttered ungraciously as she strode back to the house to shower and change.

An hour later a refreshed Nelda successfully started the pickup and was on her way to the service station to fill the gas tank. By the time she was a mile from the house, she'd decided she loved driving it. She sat up high, had good visibility, and, although her feet still barely reached the pedals, it now handled like a dream. She patted the dashboard and apologized for her earlier behavior.

"Hi," she said to the young attendant as she slid off the seat. "Fill it, please."

The boy moved leisurely to the gas pump, his eyes running the length of her trim figure in jeans and blazer.

"Got a new truck?"

"It's a loan. The garage fell on my car during the twister."

"Ya still livin' out at the farm?"

"Sure." Surprised by the question, Nelda turned and met his eyes head on. They traveled over her, then returned to her face. Nelda wanted to laugh. The kid was flirting with her! She felt the need to put him in his place. "How come you're not in school?"

"School? Ya mean college?" he drawled.

"You can't be old enough for college. I mean high school," she laughed.

The automatic gas pump clicked off, and the boy took the nozzle from the tank. While he fiddled with the gas-tank cap, Nelda went into the office and handed the cashier her credit card. She didn't see the boy again and promptly forgot all about him.

What happened at the supermarket wasn't so easily forgotten. She was pushing her cart along the frozen food section when she accidently bumped into the cart being propelled by a tall gray-haired woman.

"I'm sorry." Nelda glanced up at the woman, and their eyes met. "Mrs. Hanson?"

"Hello, Nelda." Lute's mother's tone was barely polite. "Lute mentioned you were back. Are you staying long?" Her expression plainly said that she hoped she wasn't.

"I haven't decided yet," Nelda said slowly, wishing fervently she hadn't gotten the truck started.

"If you're staying around in the hope of getting Lute back, you're wasting your time." Mrs. Hanson made her pronouncement with rocklike certainty and a faintly bitter smile.

Nelda was stung, but she maintained her composure. "What makes you say that?" she asked, hoping her eyes were hard on the older woman.

"About wasting your time? You've surely noticed that

Lute is no longer the underprivileged boy who married you due to your...promiscuous behavior. Lute won't get caught in that trap again."

The lightning bolt of pain struck an instant before thundering anger. "I didn't manage to get pregnant by myself, Mrs. Hanson. Lute realized that and insisted on shouldering his part of the responsibility, although you tried to persuade him to abandon me."

"Yes. I was against the marriage, and as it turned out, I was right. But that's all water under the bridge. What's important now is for you to get out of Lute's life and stay out. He's happy now. He has several nice women friends, and he will eventually marry one of them and raise a family."

"Are you worried that because I'm back in the area he'll change his plans? I think you're being presumptuous. If Lute fell in love and wanted to marry, I'm not sure my being here would make the slightest difference. Or would it, Mrs. Hanson?" Nelda spoke with forced bravado, but she couldn't help feeling a little victorious when a helpless look crossed the older woman's face.

"He may come to you, even spend the night as he did the other night, but he won't marry you. He loves the farm and has worked too hard to get it to leave it for any city woman." Lute's mother looked at her in a way that made her insides tie into a knot.

"I won't say it was nice to see you, Mrs. Hanson, because it wasn't. You never liked me, never gave me a chance to like you. The same went for my parents and Lute. We were two kids and easily influenced. But we're adults now and will make up our own minds about each other."

Keeping her face composed, Nelda steered her grocery cart around the woman and moved leisurely down the aisle. But out of sight behind the bread counter, she sagged against the cart. It seemed to her that all the unpleasant encounters in her life had been with her parents or Mrs. Hanson . . . all over Lute.

She quickly selected her groceries, loaded them into her cart, and wheeled it to the check-out.

Later that night she lay in the four-poster bed and thought about what Lute's mother had said. "He won't marry you. He's worked too hard to leave the farm for any city woman." Lute and his mother still thought of her as the same selfish girl she'd been long ago when she demanded that Lute leave north Iowa and go to Florida with her and her parents. Why wouldn't they think that? She cringed and felt almost sick recalling how unfair she'd been. Now Lute suspected she had come back to her grandmother's place as a lark—something of a change of pace from New York—and when the newness wore off, she would leave again. She thought long and hard about the reasons she'd come here. She had reached a crossroads in her life, and here at Grandma's she thought she could figure out what meant something and what didn't—and even maybe what she could do about it. But everything was jumbled in her head. She closed her eyes and prayed for sleep.

Despite—or maybe because of—her almost constant preoccupation with Lute, Nelda began to look forward to Saturday night and the dinner at Rhetta's. That morning she drove to the hairdresser Rhetta had recommended and emerged from the salon with her short, dark hair set in a flyaway tangle of ringlets.

Kelly was obviously unhappy to be left behind when she closed the door firmly and got into the red pickup at seven-thirty. He must have known something was up when his mistress had taken a leisurely bath and held several different outfits up for inspection before finally choosing the Jourdan suit, Nelda reflected with a chuckle.

She had needed to feel she looked her best—not that she was planning on Lute's being there, but because this

was her first social outing since she had come to north
Iowa a month ago. She knew the suit of cocoa brown
clung to her curves, and the luscious peach blouse gave
her pale, delicate skin a warm, rosy blush, bringing out
the flecks of green in her dark eyes. On impulse she had
slipped her feet into a pair of brown sandals with slender
heels and gold chains that looped around the backs of
her ankles. The shoes had been shamefully expensive,
but whenever she wore them she felt feminine and grace-
ful. She almost giggled when they pressed down on the
truck's pedals that were designed for heavy boots.

Nelda planned to arrive at Rhetta's on time, instinctively knowing that half the guests would be late and that
this way she wouldn't have to meet them all at once.
She parked the pickup alongside a long, low, dark blue
Lincoln. She whistled through her teeth when she saw
the creamy leather interior, then glanced around to see
if there were anyone to notice her incongruous gesture.

Rhetta opened the door, smiling her greeting, but once
Nelda was inside, her mouth turned down at the corners,
her expressively mobile face wry.

"Oh, dear! I swear the next friend I pick is going to
be fat and awful so I'll look good in comparison!"

Nelda found herself laughing. "You don't look exactly
dreary, yourself."

Rhetta slid a hand through Nelda's arm. "Come have
a drink and meet our crazy friend."

The man who came toward them with a drink in his
hand was about Nelda's height and had dark red hair.
He was wearing Levis and a blue cashmere sweater, but
the shoes on his feet were Gucci, and the watch on his
wrist Cartier. The jacket flung over the back of the chair
had a definite Bill Blass look. He had the face of experience that went with his forty-odd years. Here in the
heart of the corn country were all the accoutrements of
New York City, Nelda thought with some wonderment.

The bright blue eyes unabashedly assessed her and obviously approved of the quality they found in her apparel, as she had found in his. He held out his left hand and clasped hers. He raised his glass and toasted her, his blue eyes warm.

"To Nelda," he saluted before Rhetta even had a chance to make the introductions. "Will you permit me a stupid question?"

Surprised at how at ease she felt, Nelda laughed. "Sure. What's the stupid question?"

"What's a nice girl like you doing in a place like this?"

Laughing, Nelda echoed the words with him.

"A place like what?" Rhetta's snort was contemptuous. "I'll call Gary and have you thrown out, you city slicker! Are you going to let me make proper introductions, or not?"

"No, darling. We are not. This is Nelda, and I'm Norris, but I prefer to be called darling, sweetheart, lover. . . ."

"You're impossible!" The doorbell rang and Rhetta smiled. "The war's on. I hate to desert you with this wolf, Nelda, but from now on it's every woman for herself."

Norris led Nelda to the bar and made a wry face when she asked for a white wine spritzer. After Rhetta introduced the arrivals as Bill and Jean, Norris guided her to the couch and sat down beside her.

"Now, my proud beauty, as long as I'm labeled wolf I may as well act the part. What big eyes you have. No, that's the wrong line!" The friendly eyes sparkled with inner mirth. "Tell me about yourself."

"I was born in a log cabin beside a clear stream. My Pa was a poor woodsman, and my Ma took in washing," she readily ad libbed.

His laugh rang out. Nelda decided she liked him, and

during the next few minutes she framed a brief résumé of her life over the past eight years—omitting all mention of her marriage and divorce—making it sound gay and happy.

Twenty minutes later the room was awash with voices. Gary had returned from an emergency call and was telling Bill about the Arabian foal he'd delivered.

"I bloody well didn't think the old girl would make it," he said in a voice that mixed pride and relief.

Another couple arrived—Julie and Tom. She was on the plump side, and he was thin and wiry and had a G.I. crewcut. The conversation jumped from Arabian horses to firm-bodied pigs versus fat ones for sausage. Nelda was lost in the conversation. She noticed that Norris kept his eyes on her face, until a mention was made about the huge, self-propelled machines that foraged up and down the corn rows, turning dry, tattered plants into cash.

"My business," he whispered to Nelda. "I sell farm machinery."

"Oh. What kind?"

His eyes twinkled. "All kinds."

Tom and Bill, she learned, were cash grain farmers, who sold beans and saved corn for feed. Presently they were working long hours to get the crops in at just the right moisture content, aiming to beat the fall rains. They pushed hard, and when equipment failed they were cross, according to their wives, who added their bit to the conversation.

Nelda listened with envy to the two wives talking as knowledgably as their husbands about farm activities. She was the outsider here. Norris, for all his sophistication, was at least on the fringe, since his business was farm-related. Still, she was pleased that the only time he left her side was to fix himself another drink.

She was just about to relax and try to enjoy herself, sure that Lute wasn't coming, when there he was, towering in the doorway. A tall blond girl wearing a full denim skirt, her bare legs tan and shapely, was clinging to his arm.

"Hello, everybody. Sorry we're late. Lute's been busy putting up silage, and he forgot to quit," she explained with easy familiarity.

Rhetta made a strange face but commented heartily, "No harm done. I was about to pry Gary loose to put the steaks on the grill. Come meet Nelda. I think you know everyone else."

"'Course I know everyone. Hi, Julie. Hi, Jean." She then nodded to the men, her heavily mascaraed eyes focusing on each one in turn. "How are you, Mr. Smithfield?" she purred.

Although the blood was pounding in her ears, Nelda registered the name. This friendly man couldn't be *the* Smithfield, the manufacturer of farm equipment? Impossible!

"Nelda, this is Janythe Graham, the Home Economics teacher at our community high school," Rhetta spoke from beside her. "Nelda Hanson, interior decorator, late of New York, and now a permanent resident of our area— if we can convince her to stay."

"Hear! Hear!" Norris raised his glass, the others following his lead.

"Hello, Nelda." The blond girl looked at her coolly. "You have an unusual name, but I'm sure I've heard it before."

"So have you, but I'm sure I haven't heard it before," Nelda commented.

The girl laughed, but Nelda knew the battle lines were drawn. *She knows who I am, and she sees a threat,* was her reaction. That thought was quickly replaced by another when her eyes shifted to Lute and found his on her, his brows drawn together in a frown. *Yikes! Thank heavens for Norris—how would I get through this evening without him?*

The men continued to chat in spurts about the weather, crops, farm subsidies. Lute entered the conversation, virtually ignoring the girl who sat down beside him. Twenty minutes passed and Nelda hadn't added a word to the conversation, while Janythe chimed in occasionally to back up some comment of Lute's. As her morale deteriorated, Nelda began to think of escape. Because she was nervous, she had to force herself to get to her feet and walk into the kitchen in search of Rhetta. At the door she turned and saw that Lute was watching her over the rim of his glass.

"Is there anything I can do?" she asked as she spotted Rhetta standing at the microwave.

"No, but thanks. I'm trying to thaw out another steak. I didn't know the all-American girl was coming. Damn Lute! He could have called me."

"You mean they're not a steady twosome?" Nelda kicked herself mentally for asking the question.

"Jan would like them to be. She's been after him for a couple of years, now." The bell chimed and Rhetta opened the microwave door. "Thank goodness." The thawed steak she took out was enormous.

"My goodness. You don't expect each of us to eat something like that?"

"Some will, some won't. What's left the boys will eat cold. They're a couple of human garbage cans! Okay, back to the party with you. Gary will have these steaks charred in no time."

Nelda found herself sitting beside Norris during the meal. It was all very casual: picking up a steak, filling a plate from the buffet, and finding a place to eat. She and Norris shared a small, old fashioned, marble-topped ice cream table from a drug store of long ago. She remarked on the excellent condition of the antique table.

"Do you like antiques?" he queried.

"Some of them. The ones that work themselves into contemporary living."

"My sentiments exactly. How about helping me decorate my house?"

She laughed. "Just like that?"

"Why not? I'm an up-front guy." He grinned at her, his handsome face wreathed in smiles. It was a memorable face—the bones large and angular, the dark red hair disheveled in an appealing fashion, the eyes as bright as blue crystals. Her gaze lifted past his head to where Lute stood, plate in hand, looking for a place to sit. A maverick thought crossed her mind before she could capture it and wrestle it aside. *I love him, damnit*. She tore her eyes away from him.

"Thanks, but if it isn't a supper club or a suite of offices, I'm lost," she said abruptly, looking into Norris's face. He met her look with smiling eyes.

"I always wanted a suite of offices on the lakeshore," he quickly rejoined.

"You're about as obvious as a tank," she said, glancing at him sideways. She had read of Norris Smithfield's rumored sexual exploits in the gossip columns. That is, if this was really the Smithfield of farm machinery. From the conversation, she was sure he was.

He grinned at her. "I never miss an opportunity," he agreed wickedly.

"Foul creature!"

The light banter was easy for Nelda. In her line of business it was something that went along with the job. It wasn't threatening.

His eyes grew serious. "What do you find to do out at the farm all day? Don't you find it dull?"

"Dull?" She looked away, veiling her expression. She concentrated on not looking at Lute. "Dull?" she repeated, and she laughed. "I should say not! I love it. I miss the traffic, the noise, the tight schedules, and the pickpockets like I'd miss a toothache. Besides, I do get out now and then, and I've already had a flirtation with the gas station attendant."

"You what?" The words were spat out into the quiet room.

Nelda's eyes flew to Lute. His lips still parted from speaking, he was looking at her as if she'd just exploded a land mine. She felt herself flush. She knew that later, when she had time to sort things out, she'd be angry with him for forcing her to take center stage, but at the moment she felt nothing but embarrassment.

"I said I don't miss the noise, the traffic—"

"You said you had a flirtation with a gas station attendant," he interrupted. "Is that why you were so anxious to get your truck started—so you could get back to your *friend?*"

"Of course not," she retorted, uncomfortably aware of the general attention being paid her. "It was no big deal—just a kid trying to flirt with me."

"No big deal?" Lute repeated tensely. "What did he say?"

"C'mon," she said with a forced smile. "You don't expect me to remember. Boys will flirt, that's all there is to it."

"Did you enjoy it?"

Nelda checked a gasp. She wanted to laugh, or scream, but she did neither. The room was deadly quiet, everyone locked into silence by the vehemence of the exchange.

"If I did, it wouldn't be any of your business, Lute Hanson. I told you it was no big deal, so butt out!" she said indignantly.

Burning with humiliation, and surprised that she had blurted out the rude remark with such spontaneity, Nelda turned and faced Norris's twinkling eyes.

"She's right, Lute." It was Janythe's calm voice. "I imagine things like that are almost an everyday occurrence in the city. I'm sure she's old enough to handle them."

Her emphasis was decidedly on the word *old*, Nelda noticed wryly. She saw that Norris could barely contain his laughter. She giggled, too.

Janythe was speaking again. "I've been to the gas station a lot, and no one there has ever flirted with me," she was saying, implying heaven-only-knew what.

"I guess you're not as lucky as I am," Nelda said icily, turning and letting her gaze include Lute. He was still glaring at her, and her own words echoed woodenly in her ears.

Chapter

6

LATER, WHILE THE men were playing pool, Nelda had
the opportunity to apologize to Rhetta.

"I'm sorry for losing my temper with Lute and em-
barrassing your guests."

"Lute's the one who should apologize," Rhetta said
with raised eyebrows. "I've never seen him act so boor-
ish. He was like a tomcat with a sore tail." She giggled,
mischief in her eyes. "It sure didn't take the all-American
girl long to figure out you're the Nelda from Lute's past."

Past, is right. She's his future, Nelda thought wryly
on the way home. She had waited patiently until one of
the couples left, not wanting to be the one to break up
the party. She looked into the rearview mirror and saw
Norris's headlights behind her. He had insisted on following her home, although she had protested vigorously.
Before she'd gotten into the red truck she had looked
around for Lute's black pickup, but it hadn't been in the
driveway. Could the white Corvette be his? He had been
standing in front of the house with Rhetta and Gary,
Janythe clinging to his arm, when she'd pulled out of
the drive.

Nelda parked the truck behind the farmhouse and
walked back to speak to Norris, who had pulled into the
lane behind her.

"Thank you, Norris, for seeing me home."

He got out of the car and stood beside it. "My pleasure.
Shall we have dinner together some evening?"

"I'd love to. Give me a call."

"Let's make the date for tomorrow night, so I won't have to remember your number."

"I wouldn't want to put a strain on your memory, so tomorrow night it is."

Looking around before he got into his car, he suddenly asked, "What kind of protection do you have out here?"

"A good yard light, a dog, and a small handgun. I can take care of myself."

The blue eyes spoke his surprise. "Good girl. So what's between you and Lute?" he asked casually.

"I was married to him," she admitted without missing a beat.

"Oh, dear! I should have known. No wonder Miss Home Ec was in such a twist."

Nelda forced a laugh. "She's got nothing to worry about."

"Thank heavens for that!" he teased. "I'd hate to think all this hard courting I'm doing was for naught."

"You'd better go. I've got to let my dog out, and he just loves to gnaw on men with red hair and glib tongues."

Kelly was waiting for her when she opened the kitchen door. She slipped out of her shoes and fondled his ears. "Let me get out this suit, boy, and I'll take you out."

Kelly had decided of late that it was fun to roam the grove beside the house and to venture off down the road, blatantly ignoring Nelda's call to return. He had almost completely recovered from his accident, but the coddling he'd received during his convalescence had had an adverse effect on his behavior. If Nelda was out of his sight, he conveniently put her out of his mind as well, returning to the house whenever he pleased.

She slipped into her nightgown and put on her robe. "C'mon," she said to the anxious dog. "I'll wash my face later."

She stood on the steps and watched Kelly roam the yard. When she finally called, "Kelly, come," the dog

looked at her and then away. There was something outside the circle of light that needed his attention, so he
ignored her summons and disappeared around the corner
of the house. "Kelly! Damnit, Kelly!" Nelda called, then,
shivering, she stepped inside the porch to wait.

Minutes passed and the dog didn't come back. "Dumb
dog," she muttered. "Tomorrow I'm tying a rope to a
tree, and the only time you'll be outside is when you're
on the end of it!"

When headlights came up the lane she frowned, thinking Norris was returning, but the vehicle that braked
behind the pickup was a white sports car. Lute got out
with his hand firmly attached to Kelly's collar. Nelda
flung open the door, and Lute and the dog came inside.

"I found him down the road. You'd better keep him
at home, or he'll get to running with a pack. Someone
might shoot him."

Nelda had thought she was composed when Lute first
got out of the car. Now she was sure she wasn't. Her
voice trembled as she explained, "He's just started running away." Her frantic thoughts raced even as she spoke.
I can't believe he's here! What should she say, do?

Lute just stood there, looking down at her. Light from
the yard lamp illuminated the brown column of his throat
and the creases on each side of his mouth. She could
smell the peppery scent of his aftershave.

"What did you do with Miss Home Ec?" she blurted.
Oh no, had she really called her that aloud?

"I took her home," he replied without a pause.

"Don't you sleep with her?" Again she could have
kicked herself.

"What's it to you?" He looked at her hard.

She dropped her lashes, hiding her eyes. "Curious, I
guess."

"Norris Smithfield'll have *you* in bed before you know
it. Is that what you want?" he blurted angrily.

Nelda felt a shiver of warning. What was happening?

He always did something to her nerves. She lifted her
eyes to his face, probing his expression. "Lute . . ." What
she had been about to say was never said. His arms came
around her in a violent, convulsive movement, and he
held her against his hard length. She put her arms around
his neck and stretched to reach his mouth. Oh, his lips
were warm, his touch so possessive, the feel of him so
good! Pride and logic fled her mind. Lute was here. This
was now. She held his mouth with hers for a long moment, trying to memorize the feel of firm lips, silky hair,
so that when he was gone she could relive this moment
to light some lonely night.

Arms entwined, they moved into the kitchen. Lute
shut and locked the door before they climbed slowly up
the stairs to the bedroom.

She wanted to shout: "Is this all you want of me?"
hoping against hope he would respond with a passionate
declaration of undying love. But she choked it back,
knowing it was just a fantasy. She hungrily watched him
undress, then slipped out of her robe and gown.

"Nelda . . . I don't want to get you pregnant." His hands
clutched her upper arms, and he groaned the words into
her hair. "But I can't stay away from you!"

"I think it's safe, Lute."

"When are you due?" he whispered familiarly, holding
her tightly against him.

"Next week," she breathed, already lost in her need
for him.

"I didn't plan this . . . or I'd have brought . . . something."

"It'll be all right," she assured him, silently adding,
I don't want to think of anything but this, him, now.

They made love slowly, taking pleasure from every
caress. She wound her arms around him, kissing his
throat, arching responsively beneath his driving body.
Sweat glistened on his neck and dewed his back. His
hands explored her, their touch sometimes rough, but
her anxiety and anger were being released in a wild,

frenzied response, which seemed to incite him into more and more passionate lovemaking. Her pleasure erupted, and she took all he had to give, hoarding it, as if this were the final moment of her life.

She clung to him when it was over, glorying in the feel of his sweat-slick body over hers. She listened to the strains of a haunting melody in her head, knowing that, for her, nothing so beautiful could exist without love. She wondered if Lute could hear it, too. He was so gentle as he cuddled her to him that she wanted to cry. Her hand found his and touched her ring on his finger. It was so tight she couldn't even turn it.

"You could have it cut off." A tear seeped from the corner of her eye and fell onto his shoulder. He captured her hand and held it fast against his chest. "This is crazy, Lute," she whispered.

"I know." The words were a mere expulsion of breath, but his arms tightened, and he drew her legs more intimately between his.

"Do you still play the guitar?" she asked, her lips against his neck.

"Sometimes. I get together with friends and we play for a couple of hours."

"I mean by yourself. Remember when I'd rock Becky and you'd play? No matter how fussy she was, it always lulled her to sleep. I think about that sometimes. Do you ever think about that other life—when we were young and in love?"

There was a long silence. The hand holding hers to his chest moved up her arm and back in a slow rhythm. "I try not to think about that other life," he murmured into the darkness. "It's over. What's important is what's ahead."

"I like to think about it because what I was, and what I will be, is the sum total of what I am now."

"That's heavy thinking. I try to concentrate on whether or not to pick the beans, or if I have enough hail insurance, or if I'll get the crops out and still have time for fall plowing." The hand on her arm continued to stroke.

"You've always loved farming."

"Yes. I knew what I wanted to do after that first summer when I worked on one. I like working the land, watching the crops grow, caring for my animals."

"I always wanted to be a designer."

"Well," he sighed, "you got what you wanted."

"I wanted it then. Now I'm not sure what I want." She held her breath as soon as the lie left her lips. She knew what she wanted: she'd walk over hot coals to be with him; he had only to beckon. "I don't know what to do about Grandpa's farm." She rushed into speech before he could comment on her remark. "I can't decide if I should sell it or hold onto it for an investment."

"You can always lease out the land, but if the house isn't lived in, it'll deteriorate."

There was a long silence. She turned her lips to the warm skin of his chest and choked down the disappointment she felt when he let the subject of selling the farm drop so blandly.

"Why haven't you ever remarried, Lute?"

"Why haven't you?"

"I don't know. Too busy with my job, I guess." She took a quivering breath. "Janythe Graham seems perfect for you."

"Yes. She'd make a good wife for a farmer," he acknowledged.

"And I wouldn't." The words were out before she could stop them.

"No. I can't see you as the Florence Nightingale of the calf barn, or being concerned with anything as unglamorous as corn and soybeans. I realized that more clearly tonight when I saw you with Smithfield. You fit into his world much better than you do mine." The hand now gripped hers tightly.

"Then why did you come here?" Hurt made her speak sharply.

"You know why."

"What does that make me, Lute?" she challenged.

"It makes you the most beautiful, desirable woman I've ever known. It makes me want to grab you whenever I see you and lose myself in you. No woman feels like you feel, smells like you smell, tastes like you taste." He pulled her on top of him. "Love me again. Take me to heaven one more time." The words were a husky plea.

She wanted to shout and scream for him to get the hell out, to stop torturing her. Instead, she kissed him, caressed him, made sweet, slow motions over his body, trying not to rush, trying to make him hear her heart's song. It was over too soon, and she nestled in his arms and listened to the steady beat of his heart while he slept.

In the morning, Lute slipped out of the warm bed without a word or a touch. He simply untangled his limbs from hers and swung them over the side of the bed. Nelda watched him dress as the cold dawn invaded the bedroom.

He paused at the door when she called his name, then walked back to the middle of the room, where her next words stopped him. "Will you be back?"

He looked at her for a full minute, then walked out without answering. Kelly followed him downstairs, then returned to his rug beside the bed when the sound of Lute's Corvette died away.

The next few weeks passed so quickly that Nelda wondered later how she had filled them. She had plunged into the work of getting screens ready for block printing some scarves she wanted to make. After she made several trips to Mason City, the porch was littered with cans of textile dye and screens set around a table equipped with the frame and clamps for holding the cloth. Her art work had been completed, and now she was down to the next part of the project.

She'd also had several dates with Norris, and found him to be an enjoyable companion. Outside of a few chaste kisses when he brought her home, he had made no move to plunge their friendship into an affair. Nelda strongly suspected that the image he projected was a cover up for a man who was lonely—who missed the children who remained with their mother after his divorce, and who knew their father mostly as the man who sent support money.

Every day until late at night she could hear the sound of farm machinery in the fields surrounding the house. The rush was on to get the harvest in before snowfall; tractors pulling up to three and four grain wagons passed the house daily on the way to the elevator. The black-topped roads leading into town were choked with semi-trucks and wagons filled with shelled corn waiting to be unloaded. Not wanting to have to pass long lines of trucks on blind curves—or to travel at their slow pace—Nelda started driving around her section of land to reach the highway. In so doing she had to pass Lute's house.

The house was huge, fronting on a wide lawn that sloped down to the road. His mailbox was set atop a freshly painted post surrounded by hollyhock stalks, now dried by the killing frosts. The storm windows were already up, and a dried arrangement of Indian corn hung on the door. After the first time, Nelda didn't look at the house when she passed, lest she see Janythe Graham there.

On one of her long daily walks with Kelly she paused to watch a huge machine pulling a wagon across one of the fields. The machine's large spout was spitting shelled corn into the wagon. When it was filled, a second wagon was hitched to the cornpicker and the process began again. Nelda stood leaning on a fence, fascinated by the mechanical rhythm. When the gigantic machine reached the end of the row near the fence, she saw Lute's blond head through the cab window. A fierce joy pounded in her blood, causing her heart to race. The picker swung around to start back down the rows, then stopped. Lute opened the door of the cab and jumped down.

In worn jeans and a denim jacket, he was so handsomely masculine that Nelda could hardly take her eyes off him. Kelly whined and wiggled a welcome, and Lute stooped to poke his fingers through the fence and scratch behind the dog's ears.

"Hi. Nice day," he yelled over the engine's roar. "If the weather holds I'll get this field picked by evening." She barely heard his words, but she recognized he was being friendly. Her heart danced happily in her breast.

"Looks like it could snow," she shouted.

"Would you like to make a trip across the field and back?"

"I'd love to, but what about Kelly?"

"Tie him to the fence. He'll be okay."

Lute grabbed hold of a fence post, stuck his booted toe in one of the wire squares, and jumped over. He took Kelly's leash from her hand and tied it to the pole. The dog barked his resentment at being left behind. Lute jumped back over the fence and stood waiting for Nelda.

"I don't know if I can do it," she laughed.

Lute grinned. "Sure you can. Put your foot on the wire and grab the post."

Determined to try, Nelda did as she was told, but the fence was too high for her, and she ended up helplessly suspended, a leg dangling on either side.

"What'll I do? The barb at the top has caught my jeans," she yelled.

"You're in a hell of a mess," Lute laughed. "Maybe I should leave you there—you'd make a damned attractive scarecrow."

"Lute! You buzzard! Help me!"

He stood laughing merrily at her predicament.

"Get me off of here!" she wailed.

He came to her, and his hands circled her waist. "It was fun while it lasted—the chic Ms. Hanson classing up a cornfield."

She ignored his taunting flattery—and tried to ignore the pounding of her heart as she felt his grip on her waist and dropped her hands to his shoulders. He lifted her until she leaned against him, then reached around her to unhook her jeans from the barbed strand of wire. Try not to clutch at him, she commanded herself. Act as though it's no earthshaking event to be so close to him. She slid down the solid length of him until her feet touched the ground. Her arms were still about his neck when she looked up. She was surprised by the look of tight emotion on his face. She tried to turn away quickly, but his fingers beneath her chin lifted her face toward his and he kissed her lips gently. She responded with trepidation, then with warmth, her arms tighter about his neck, pulling him closer to her. He slid one hand down to her hips, then up under her jacket. As his hand captured a breast, his breathing quickened and his kiss deepened. Longing swamped her, and she pressed desperately into his embrace.

Abruptly he pulled away, turning and striding to the picker. Panic and confusion tore at her heart. He acts as if he's angry because he kissed me, she thought. One moment of sweet sharing, the next moment rebuff. She trailed him to the tractor, and Lute flung open the door. The step up was enormous, and Nelda glanced at Lute with a nervous smile. He wasn't smiling. His brows were knit together, and she desperately wished she had refused to come. Lute sprang lightly into the cab, then reached down for her hand. She put her booted foot on the step, and he hauled her up beside him, simultaneously flipping down a folded, padded seat.

The interior of the cab was almost as plush as his pickup truck, she noted. Huddled on the small passenger

chair, Nelda watched Lute settle himself into the con-
toured seat behind the wheel. His gloved hands worked
the controls of the powerful machine, and it began to
move. The sound of the engine was muffled inside the
cab, competing only with the soft stereo music.

"Is this the kind of machine Norris makes?" Nelda
asked to have something to say.

"No. This particular one is made by his competitor,
but I do have one of his." Lute steered between the rows
of dried corn stalks, and Nelda watched as their vehicle
seemed to swallow them. She saw him glance from time
to time into the large mirror to watch the shelled corn
spew out of the funnel and into the wagon behind.

"What happens to the corncob?" she queried, genu-
inely curious.

"It's chewed up and left in the field." He looked at
her. "Earlier, before the frost, we cut some of the green
stalks, grind them up for winter feed, and put them in
the silo," he explained, almost grudgingly she thought.

At the end of the field they stopped and waited while
a small tractor took away their loaded wagon and hitched
up an empty one. Lute didn't speak again, and his fingers
drummed impatiently on the steering wheel.

Why is he acting like this? Nelda fretted. He's sorry
he asked me to come. *Oh, Lute, darling, don't shut me
out! I can share your life. I know I can.*

"I've started making my block prints," she volunteered. She had to make him talk to her. In a few short
minutes they would be back at the fence where they'd
left Kelly—and she probably wouldn't see him again for
weeks. "I had my screens burned in Mason City," she
continued. "I think you'd like my designs, Lute. They're
earthy." She laughed nervously. "Corn, milkweed pods,
even thistle."

"Thistle? How strange to find something pretty about
a thistle. We have to spray constantly to keep them out
of the fields."

His words were cynical, and they hurt, but she thought she detected a pensive note in his voice. Uneasy silence hung between them. Uncertain how to deal with his moodiness, she tried to keep a tremor from her voice as she acknowledged, "I didn't realize that."

"I'm sure you didn't," he said, and this time there was no mistaking the cynicism in his voice.

Nelda drew in a deep breath. They reached the end of the field, and Lute swung the machine in a wide arc, stopping beside the fence. Kelly barked and wiggled and tried to get through the small wire squares to reach them. Lute opened the cab door, jumped down, then reached for her. She put her hands on his shoulders, and her eyes clung to his face.

He swung her down gently, muttering, "Not as exciting as a taxi ride in New York, but it's all we've got to offer."

"It was wonderful. I loved it. Thank you, Lute," she protested sincerely into his dark expression. Why did it have to be like this? She started to move away, but he grabbed her roughly and pulled her back to him.

"You forgot to pay the driver."

He crushed her to him so hard the air exploded from her lungs. His mouth found hers and mastered it almost cruelly. He kissed her long and hard. His hands gripped her ruthlessly, almost as though he wanted to hurt her, but gradually they gentled and roved over her slowly, and his lips softened when he kissed her again. Nelda forced herself to stand quietly in his embrace, straining to conceal the wild, tremulous sensations that quivered into being beneath the adventuring hands that slid beneath her jacket to cup her breasts until her nipples were hard in his fingers. Presently he loosened his arms, gently pushing her away from him.

"Go," he said tiredly. "I've got work to do."

She left him without a backward glance, but she knew he watched as she climbed back over the fence. She managed to reach the other side without a hitch, untied Kelly, and walked swiftly down the road. Behind her she heard the tractor pulling the cornpicker roar into action.

During the next few weeks a sort of peace settled over Nelda. A wonderful revelation had changed her outlook on life completely. She was pregnant. It was not confirmed, but after two missed periods and a week of morning sickness, she was sure that by next May she would have Lute's baby. This time there was no fear of facing her parents—her father was virtually a distant relation—and no problem of money. She didn't have to worry whether or not Lute would marry her. He would if he knew she was carrying his child—she was sure of it. But he need never know that the seed he had planted would blossom into life come spring. The whole scenario of their life would be played over again if he knew. He would be caught in the same bind! Never, she vowed. Even if he'd wanted her for a wife back then, he certainly didn't now.

Most of Nelda's waking hours were now spent in planning a future for herself and her child. Many single women raised children alone, she reasoned, and she welcomed the responsibility. She would sell the farm, invest the money, and that, along with the inheritance she had received from her mother, would give her a modest income. She would find a place in a medium-sized town, maybe somewhere in the southwest, and make a life for herself and her child. She could try to make a go of textile designing, but if that didn't work she could fall back on interior decorating.

It crossed Nelda's mind several times that it was unfair of her not to tell Lute about his son or daughter, whichever it might be. But weighing that unfairness against the fact that Lute didn't love her—only desired her because they were so compatible in bed, and would honorably marry her while thinking her totally unsuitable for rural life—she knew she had made the right decision. Lute would never believe that her career could come second to her life with him on the farm. He'd never believe that she could adapt to country living, only occasionally traveling to the city to keep her hand in the field of interior and textile design. Worse, she sensed he didn't *want* to believe it. He wanted to shut her out of his life the way he must have thought she had. He'd been stubborn as a boy—as a man he was obdurate, unforgiving. It was *her* problem that she'd found him again and confirmed that she still loved him. Loved him— Lute, the man—not just her romantic memory of a sensitive boy.

She tried dreadfully hard to close out thoughts of the years ahead without him, hoping that somehow it would be slightly easier now that his child would be with her. . . .

Rhetta proved to be a good friend. She nudged and pushed until Nelda took on a few hours of volunteer work at the library, delivered Meals on Wheels for a week to the shut-ins, and even addressed envelopes for the swimming pool committee when they sent out a mailing requesting donations. But she absolutely drew the line when Rhetta tried to get her involved in politics.

"But we need someone like you on our central committee," Rhetta pleaded. "All our members are so old and set in their ways, they wouldn't recognize a new idea if it hit them in the face."

Nelda stayed firm and resisted her friend's pleas. To make up for it she agreed to a shopping trip to Minneapolis. It was one of the most enjoyable days she'd had in a long while. They shopped, lunched, and shopped again. Nelda bought running shoes because they were so comfy, then laughingly asked the salesman if she could walk in them since running wasn't her thing. Rhetta insisted that she would need fur-lined boots for winter.

Nelda knew she wouldn't be needing them—that she'd be long gone by then—but she bought them to placate Rhetta. While her friend was buying sweaters for her boys, Nelda visited the bookstore and came away with a shopping bag full of paperback novels. Hidden beneath the pile were books on prenatal care and how to raise a baby. She even bought a pattern book for knitting baby garments.

The secret of her pregnancy was so sweet in Nelda's mind that it helped hold thoughts of Lute at bay. She was resigned to the fact that she couldn't have him—that he desired her body, but didn't, couldn't, love her whole self. So she made her plans carefully, pacing herself, knowing she would be able to stay in Iowa until after Thanksgiving. Then she would make a business trip and never return.

Halloween came and went. Preoccupied with her designs and her volunteer work, Nelda would scarcely have known about it were it not for the soap marks that appeared on the library windows. She loved the time she spent in the library. Her hours were from eleven until one o'clock, well after her morning sickness had passed, and there were few visitors at that time. She browsed to her heart's content among the baby books, reading up on childhood diseases and the like. She was sure eyebrows would be raised if she checked them out, so she contented herself with poring over them during her volunteer hours.

The first week of November it snowed. Nelda got up one morning to see the ground covered in white and the fluffy flakes still drifting down. Her first thought was of Lute and if he had gotten all his crops out.

In the middle of the morning Norris called.

"You're back!" she greeted him happily. "Did you turn the manufacturing world inside out with my idea to paint all your farm machinery robin's egg blue?"

He laughed. "No. But they were still considering your

idea of covering them with art deco tulip decals. Did you miss me?"

"Grieved every hour you were away."

"If only that were true," he groaned. "How about going cross-country skiing with me?"

"When, where, and how? I don't have skis."

"Now. At your place or mine, and I have skis."

"Make it this afternoon, here, and you've got a date."

"I'll be there at two o'clock."

"I've got chili in the crockpot."

"I'll bring a huge appetite."

The temperature was only ten above zero, but on the snowmobile trail in the woods, sheltered from the wind, Nelda found herself sweating from the exertion of shuffling the light skis over the loose snow. She pulled off her muffler, and then, still too warm, partially unzipped her down jacket. The feel of cold air rushing against her throat and chest was exhilarating.

She followed along behind Norris, who held his pace to accommodate hers, until they reached the crest of a hill and surveyed the countryside below. Spread before them was a panorama of farmhouses surrounded by windbreaks—tightly branched black pine trees all lined up in orderly rows along the property squares. Nelda's eyes quickly singled out Lute's house and dwelled there for a long moment. To the southeast they could see the tall, rounded, concrete silos of the grain elevator. The scene was all shades of green on white, white on white, interrupted only by an occasional red barn.

Norris was silent while they rested, and Nelda was consumed by an emotion she didn't often feel; a feeling of belonging. She loved this place, this life, this view. Dear God, she thought, soon I'll be leaving it forever. But I'll return to it often in my mind.

"You okay?" Norris had moved up beside her and was peering into her face.

"Sure."

He reached out and zipped up her jacket, winding the muffler about her neck. "Let's go home and eat that chili."

Home. There was that word again. Not too long ago she'd thought that Iowa and her grandparents' farmhouse might become her home. Now she didn't know just where her home might be. *Let's go home.* The words had rolled so easily off Norris's tongue, but they had little meaning that way. If only it were Lute saying those words to her . . .

Guiltily bringing her attention back to Norris, she inwardly acknowledged how grateful she was for his friendship at this particular time in her life. She also unhappily acknowledged that her heart would forever belong to Lute, even if he didn't want it. Sometimes in the dark of night she would be so lonely for him, and the thought of the years ahead without him would be so painful, that she wondered if it might be better to die than to feel this way. Then thoughts of the baby would corral her reckless musings back into perspective, and she would begin planning for the future once again.

Realizing that she'd again drifted off into dreaming of Lute, she plunged her ski poles into the snow and pushed off. The vigorous exercise felt good. Sometimes as they moved lightly over the snow, the silence complete, they seemed to be in another world. Nelda laughed aloud when she scared up a jack rabbit, who went bounding helter-skelter over the pristine white landscape. One time she fell and lay sprawled in the light, fluffy, whipped-cream snow until Norris heard her laughing and returned to help her back onto her skis.

Kelly was delighted to see them when they returned, and Norris frolicked with him in the snow until Nelda called the two playmates in for dinner.

After the meal she beat Norris soundly at a game of Scrabble, then accused him of being a poor loser when he refused a rematch.

"How about blackjack?" he asked hopefully.

"Sure, but I remember cards and you wouldn't stand a chance."

"I detest smart women," he teased, scanning her small library and selecting several books. "I've always wanted to know about prenatal care, the care and feeding of an infant from birth to six months, and how to toilet train a child with a minimum of fuss."

"Oh, no!"

The bright blue eyes focused on her flushed face. She sat immobile, watching him.

"You're pregnant."

"Oh, no!" she groaned at him for knowing.

"It wasn't awfully hard to figure out." He carefully replaced the books and came to sit down beside her. "Is it something you wanted to happen?"

"Not wanted, but now that it did, I'm glad."

"It's Lute's, of course. Does he know?"

"No! And he mustn't know!"

"Why not? You love him."

She momentarily raged inside. "Where do you get off knowing so much about me?"

He smiled at her anger, and his hand came out to clasp hers. "It was obvious to me the night I met you."

"Oh . . ." she wailed.

He laughed. "Don't worry. You hid it well. But I'm Norris, the womanizer, remember? It's my predatory nature to know if a woman will go to bed with me, or if she's pining for another man, or if she'll go to bed with me in spite of the fact that she's in love with another man and wants to try and get him out of her system."

Nelda put her fingers over his lips, and he drew her head down onto his shoulder.

"You're not like that at all, Norris Smithfield," she protested.

"How long will you stay here?" he asked quietly.

"Until Thanksgiving."

"When do you expect the baby?"

"In May." She held tightly to him, then peeled herself away and looked at him for a long, agonizing moment. "I'm going to have a baby. It's so good to say it out loud. Thank you, Norris."

"How about that! I've turned into a shrink!" He kissed the tip of her nose. "Now pay me my fifty bucks and I'll get the hell out of here."

"I think I love you, Norris."

"Yeah. Like a favorite uncle," he groaned.

"Something like that, you fraud!"

She stood at the door and watched him brush the snow from the windshield of his car. He started the motor and set the wipers moving, then came back to the porch.

"I'm going to Minneapolis at the end of the week."

Nelda drew her bottom lip between her teeth. "How about hooking a ride? I hate driving in this stuff."

"Sure. It'll be a one-day trip. Will Kelly be okay for a day?"

"He won't like it, but he'll be okay. I want to see an obstetrician."

"Know one?"

"No, but . . ."

"I've got a friend in Minneapolis. Would you like for me to ask her to make an appointment for you?"

"I'd appreciate it," she said softly.

"No problem. I'll give you a call after I talk to her."

True to her premonition in the cornfield, Nelda hadn't seen Lute for a month, but she saw him the morning she and Norris left to go to Minneapolis. It was barely eight A.M. when Norris stopped the car at the end of the lane to let the black pickup pass. He tooted the horn and waved. Lute lifted his hand from the wheel in a salute. The glimpse she had of his set face lasted only a few seconds, but the image stayed in her mind all day.

Lute thought Norris had spent the night with her!

Chapter

7

It was a thirty-minute flight to Minneapolis in the chartered plane, and a forty-five minute drive in the rented car to Norris's apartment from the airport.

"Your appointment is for eleven. I'll have you there in plenty of time," he said with confidence.

The car dodged into a lane of traffic, swung off the freeway, and made its way down a tree-lined street of ultra-modern buildings. They pulled into a circular drive and parked.

The inside of the Norris's building fairly screamed affluence. In the elevator, he inserted a key and the cage moved. In mere seconds it slid to a gentle stop and the door opened.

The apartment was elegant but also comfortable. Nelda slipped out of her cashmere coat and removed her hat and gloves when Norris invited her to make herself comfortable.

"I've some calls to make," he explained. "There should be snacks in the kitchen if you're hungry. Lots of dill pickles and peanut butter." He grinned at her.

"Oh, hush and make your calls before I throw up all over your lovely carpet!"

He disappeared into another part of the apartment, and she looked with interest at the tastefully decorated room. Norris probably employed a live-in housekeeper, or else one who came in daily. The many plants, which were set in just the right places, would need constant care. The pale green silk-covered sofa and matching pillows, the Louis XV chairs, the tables with delicately carved legs and the silk-shaded lamps were all perfect, just the right setting for a man like Norris. But not for Lute . . . or for her, the thought popped unbidden into her mind.

She wandered down the hall and found a bathroom. When she came out she turned toward the kitchen and heard Norris's voice coming from another room.

"I'm sorry, darling. I couldn't reach you last night. Won't you try to come over?" He paused. "Then meet us for lunch. . . . All right, we'll meet you here at two o'clock. Is everything okay? Jenny, too? I'm glad you finally got over the flu . . ."

Nelda slipped by the door and returned to the living room. Obviously Norris was talking with someone he cared very much about. He seldom mentioned anyone except his two daughters, both college students, who attended school in California, but it wasn't one of them. He returned to the living room in high spirits, and they left for the doctor's office.

Norris let Nelda out of the car in front of the medical building without mentioning the two o'clock appointment back at the apartment. "I'll park the car and wait for you in the lobby. You have the card? Okay. Don't be nervous. You'll like this doctor. Every pregnant woman I bring to him falls in love with him." She knew he was trying to tease the serious look from her face.

Nelda walked into the building smiling. She didn't need him to lift her spirits. She was already comfortable with the idea that she was going to have a baby—and confident she'd be able to handle rearing one as a single parent. Despite her small bone structure she had borne one child, and she could do so again.

Later, over lunch at a small café near the medical building, she was telling Norris about the doctor. "I like him. I'd planned to go back to New York, or somewhere in the southwest, but I may stay here until after the baby comes." She sank into deep thought. "I can work on my prints here as easily as anywhere else, I guess."

Norris looked at his watch. "Do you have any prescriptions to be filled?"

"I'm afraid so," she said apologetically.

He covered her hand. "No problem. We'll do it on the way back to the apartment. There's someone coming over I'd like you to meet." There seemed to be a special brightness in his blue eyes. He's in love with this woman, Nelda thought. Hopelessly in love with her.

Aloud she said, "I hope you're not trying to fix me up with some friend of yours!"

"Hardly, sweetheart." He laughed and helped her up from the booth. "You've already been fixed up, or had you forgotten?"

"That was crude!" she complained while he was fumbling for money to pay the bill.

"Yeah. Come to think of it, it was," he said laughing. "But I thought it was rather clever."

"You would," she retorted, pretending huffiness.

The lamps were lit and the stereo was playing softly when they reached the apartment. Norris helped Nelda with her coat, placed it carefully over the back of a chair, then excused himself and walked quickly toward the back of the apartment.

Nelda walked over to the window and looked down onto the busy street. The thought of returning to New York, or going somewhere totally unknown in the southwest, had never been a pleasant one, she finally admitted to herself. Now she was thinking she could come to Minneapolis, start her new life here. As long as he didn't know, she could be as removed from Lute as if she were two thousand miles away.

"Nelda."

She turned to face Norris and the woman at his side. She hoped her surprise wasn't written on her face. This was hardly the sleek, sophisticated type the world would expect Norris Smithfield to be attracted to, but rather a lovely, mature woman with soft, dark hair. She was not yet middle-aged, but she was no longer young. There were tiny lines at the corners of her haunting green eyes and her full, generous mouth. She was slender, yet the soft silk of her dress showed her to be rounded and sweetly feminine.

Norris was looking at the woman with a happy smile in his eyes, as if she were something infinitely precious. If Lute ever looked at me like that, Nelda thought wistfully, I'd melt away.

"Nelda Hanson and Marlene Lindon, I'd like for you two ladies to know each other."

"Hello, Marlene." Nelda held out her hand.

"Hello, Nelda. It's nice to meet you." Marlene's handshake was firm.

"Thank you, it's nice to meet you, too."

"Now that we've gotten that over with, let's have some coffee," Norris exclaimed without ceremony. He was practically beaming with pride. He put his hand gently on Marlene's back and urged her toward the kitchen. "C'mon, Chicken Little," he said to Nelda. "We'll have the orgy in the kitchen."

"Norris!" Marlene chided gently, then stage-whispered to Nelda, "I suppose you're used to him by now, and you know that *he's* really the Chicken Little."

"Oh, yes. He already knows I know he's a fraud!"

"I'm not sure I like having my two favorite women talking about me as if I were a naughty child." Norris tried to frown, but it turned into a happy grin. "What's in the box, honey?" He reached out an arm and hooked it about Marlene, as if compelled to touch her constantly.

"Swedish coffee cake, and you must share it with Nelda. She can use the extra calories."

"And I suppose I can't?" Norris protested in a wounded tone.

"You know you can't," Marlene countered with easy familiarity.

Nelda watched and smiled and felt something a little bit like envy. It was so beautiful, so rare.

They spent a pleasant hour. Norris made no effort to conceal the fact that he was desperately in love with Marlene. She, in turn, seemed totally happy to be with him. Nelda realized their relationship was not a new thing when Norris mentioned Marlene's daughter, Jenny, who was starting her first year in college.

"She's going to be every bit as pretty as her mother, though I didn't think so when she was going through that gawky stage."

Marlene positively glowed when she looked at Norris. Her face had a soft, luminous beauty, and her eyes held a kind of passionate tenderness. Nelda wondered if Marlene knew about her and why she was here. Her next words told Nelda that Norris had no secrets from her.

"What did Doctor Wilkins say? Do you like him?"

The rest of the time was spent talking about her condition and how she felt about having the baby. No mention was made of the baby's father, but somehow Nelda knew that Norris had discussed that with Marlene, too. She felt no resentment—she instinctively knew that Marlene could be trusted. Just before it was time to leave for the airport, Nelda excused herself and spent a good long while in the bathroom to give the couple some time alone.

Marlene walked with them to the elevator. "I'll tidy up before I leave. No need for maid service to do it." She reached for Nelda and gave her a gentle hug. "When you come back to Minneapolis, give me a call. I know you're going to be just fine under Doctor Wilkins's care, but if you need a friend in the city, I'd like to apply for the position."

Norris put his arms around the calm, beautiful woman and kissed her tenderly. "I'll call you tonight, darling. Take care."

They were silent as they drove out of the city toward

the airport. Norris seemed to be wrapped up in his own thoughts, and Nelda was reluctant to break into them. Finally he turned and smiled tightly at her.

"Thank you for letting me meet Marlene," Nelda said. "She's lovely."

"Yes, she's lovely, sweet, compassionate—she's all things to me. I love her more than life. She's the reason I live in Iowa part of the time. I couldn't bear to be with her all the time and not have her."

"Oh... I'm sorry."

"She's married," he said, keeping his eyes straight ahead. "Her husband was in a plane crash and has extensive brain damage. He'll never recover, but he's been kept alive in a care facility, and she'll never divorce him."

"Have you known her long?"

"Eight years."

Eight years, the same length of time that I've been alone, she thought. But now, she reminded herself, with Lute's baby growing inside her, she was no longer alone.

It was after dark when they reached the farmhouse. The weather had worsened: a thin rain had fallen, coating everything with a solid sheet of ice. Norris headed into the house with Nelda and caught her in his arms when she slipped on the glazed concrete steps.

"You stay in the house, young lady," he ordered sternly. "I'll tie Kelly's rope so it's long enough for him to come up onto the porch, and you can hook him up and unhook him there. You stay off those steps until I bring out some sand."

"Yes, Uncle Norris!" She laughed and kissed him on the cheek. "I wonder what Rhetta and the others would think if they knew you aren't the lecher you pretend to be."

"Give away my secret and I'll...punch you in the nose."

* * *

The next week brought a warming trend that melted the ice and made it fairly easy to get around again. Nelda worked her three days at the library, and on her way home occasionally stopped at a fast-food place on the highway so she wouldn't have to cook a meal. One evening she pulled in beside a black pickup with a red interior, and, rather than take the chance of running into Lute, she backed out and drove through the takeout lane. When she pulled up to the traffic light at the exit to the highway, the black pickup with Lute and Janythe Graham pulled up beside her. Janythe waved, and Nelda lifted a heavy hand in acknowledgment. That night she started packing the things she would take with her when she moved to Minneapolis.

Rhetta invited her over often. Although she didn't come right out and say so, she clearly didn't understand or approve of Nelda's friendship with Norris Smithfield. She brought up Lute's name several times in conversation: Lute and the boys had been pheasant hunting, Lute and Gary were going to Wyoming to hunt deer when the season opened, Lute had bought a block of tickets to the Harvest Ball, which was a benefit for the swimming pool project.

Nelda read in the weekly newspaper the list of local residents who had gone south for the winter. Lute's mother's name was there. I bet she hated to go away with me here, Nelda mused. If she only knew how little she had to worry about. Oh, Baby, Baby, she thought desperately, resting her hand on her slightly rounded stomach, if not for you I just might lose my mind!

During the day fresh snow had whitened the landscape. Now the moon shone brightly, making the countryside look like a fairyland. Nelda put on her coat and stood on the porch watching Kelly frolic in the snow on the end of his rope. She doubted he would run away if she turned him loose—he seemed to prefer lying on the warm rug beside the hot air register these days—but she didn't want to risk having to get the car out to go look for him. It was a beautiful night, the air still, cold, and crystal clear. She hugged her arms to herself, called Kelly in, and prepared to turn in for the night.

Later, lying in bed with a novel, she heard the sound of snowmobiles coming down the road. A perfect night for a ride, she thought, and she switched off the bedside lamp so she could stand at the window and watch them pass. To her surprise, the lead machine turned up the lane toward the house and five others followed.

Company at this time of night? The illuminated clock said it was after midnight. Who would it possibly be? She grabbed her flannel robe and slid her feet into slippers. The nightlight burning in the hall was all she needed to see her way down the stairs. Kelly barked, and she put her hand on his head to quiet him. He growled, and she shushed him. She moved over to the back door, testing it to be sure it was locked, then parted the curtain and looked out. The six machines were in the yard, their lights turned off.

"Come join the party. We know you're home. We saw the light." The voice was young and male.

"Come out, come out, wherever you are." Giggles and shouts followed this remark.

The figures moving around the yard in snowmobile suits and helmets looked like moon-walkers. Nelda saw a glint as one tipped a bottle to his lips and another jerked it out of his hand. The yard light shining on the snow made an area almost as light as day out of the surrounding darkness. The invaders all seemed to be high-school age or slightly older.

Nelda was nervous, but not terribly so until one of the youths came up to the back porch and perched on the steps. Then her heart jumped into her throat and began a wild gallop. She backed away from the door and felt along the cabinets to the telephone. She lifted the receiver and dialed *O*.

"Operator, will you please ring the sheriff for me? There are intruders in my yard. I'd look up the number, but I don't dare turn on a light."

"I understand. Hold on."

"Sheriff's office."

"This is Nelda Hanson, and I live on the Severt Hansen place, one mile north of County Road E. There's a gang of six boys on snowmobiles in my yard, and I think they're drunk."

"Have they tried to get into the house?"

"Not yet. But they have no business being on my property."

"I don't think you need be alarmed. It's just some kids having a party. The high school team won the right to play in the state football championships. They're out celebrating. Kids are having parties all over the county. I don't have a car in your vicinity, but when I do I'll have him drive around your way. Just keep the door locked. You'll be all right."

"Thanks a lot!" Nelda slammed down the phone.

"One, two three, charge!" The singsong voice came from just below the steps.

"You guys are nuts! You tryin' to scare that woman?"

"Oh, shut up, chicken," another voice called.

"Yip . . . yip . . . ooo . . ."

That set off a chorus of yipping, and Nelda became so frightened she was almost sick. She picked up the phone again and started to feel her way around the dial to call Norris. Then she remembered—he was in Chicago! Whom to call? What to do? One thing was sure, she couldn't depend on the sheriff. As drunk as those kids are, they just might try to break into the house! They might hurt the baby! Fear as cold as ice traveled the length of her spine. She hurried up the stairs to her room and got her pistol from the bureau drawer, slipped it into her pocket, and hurried back down the stairs again. She watched the gang from the kitchen window. They were bunched in front of the back steps, talking in low voices. Suddenly the huddle broke up, and they began to pound each other on the back. One youth came onto the porch and held the door so the others couldn't follow.

Without hesitation, Nelda went to the phone again.

"Operator, I'm so scared I don't know what to do. Please call Lute Hanson on Route Two for me. He's my nearest neighbor, and I need help."

The phone rang four times before Lute answered it.

"Lute, this is Nelda. There're six boys in my yard. One is up on the porch. They're drunk, and I don't know what to do. The sheriff won't come, but I've got a gun, and I'll shoot if they try to come into the house!"

"My God! Don't do anything. If you think they're going to come in, go to the basement and get into the bin where your Grandpa kept coal. Before they find you I'll be there. For God's sake, be careful with that gun!"

She held the phone for a few seconds after it went dead. Tears were running down her cheeks. Lute would come! She stood with her back to the basement door, her knees trembling. Kelly stood cowering against her legs. Laughter on the porch! Was it the voice of the kid from the filling station? The one she'd put down when he'd flirted with her? Oh, Lute! Please hurry!

"Old chicken is leavin'. Cluck, cluck, cluck . . ." The sound of one of the machines being started reached Nelda's ears, then the muffled purr as it shot off down the lane. Some of the boys were still making clucking noises after their departing friend.

"Hey! Here comes someone. Whoa! Look at that fool drive!"

The relief Nelda felt was quickly replaced by fear for Lute. He was one against five! She gripped the small pistol and inched over to the window. Only two of the youths were beside the back steps, the others had hurried to their machines.

"Oh no! It's Lute Hanson. How'd he . . ."

The black pickup slammed to a stop, and Lute shot out the door.

"What the hell is going on here?" he roared.

"Hi, Lute. We was just havin' a little beer bust."

"We wasn't hurtin' nothin', Lute, we—"

"We were just horsing around, and—"

"Horsing around on someone else's property is a good way to get your heads blown off!" Lute said angrily. "Now get the hell away from here. If you've got to act like fools, do it on my property, or somewhere where folks won't think you're a gang of hoodlums intending to break in."

Two of the youths mounted their machines and started them up, heading out to go down the lane.

"All right. The rest of you scatter! I'll talk with you later about this."

"Ah, Lute! You tell 'bout this and we'll get thrown off the team," one of them whined.

Nelda turned on the kitchen light and unlocked the door. She stepped out onto the porch.

"Lute, I want to see what they look like. I want to know if I've seen them before," she called.

"Let it go, Nelda," Lute said briskly. "Get out of here, you guys, and count yourselves lucky."

Nelda went back into the kitchen, sat down at the table, and rested her head on her arms. She felt sick. She heard the machines start, then the roar as they sped across the yard on the way to the road. Reaction set in, and she began to shake.

Chapter

8

LUTE OPENED THE door and Kelly was there to greet him, obviously delighted, wiggling appreciatively when Lute fondled his ears. It took several seconds for Nelda's eyes to focus on his face. He stood just inside the door, his hair tousled, a faint stubble of beard on his cheeks.

"Are you all right?" he asked.

She nodded. "Thanks for coming. I tried to get the sheriff to come out, but he didn't seem to think it was much of an emergency."

"I know those kids," Lute said slowly. "I can't believe they meant to break into the house. They'd been drinking a bit, raising a little hell, and I doubt if they gave a thought that they might be scaring you. I'll admit it was a dumb idea, but my word! If you'd shot one of them . . ."

Nelda began to laugh. "You and the sheriff! Can't you get it into your heads that this is my property, and they had no right to come here in the middle of the night scaring me to death!" she shouted. "Your good old country boys were just out 'horsing around.' Well, let me tell you, Mr. Lute Hanson, that fifty percent of all crimes in the United States are committed by boys that age. If anyone tries to break into this house, they're in for a surprise. I've got my gun, and I know how to use it. At least I could call the police in New York, and they wouldn't treat me like some hysterical old maid!" she babbled. Tears flowed down her cheeks. "Now you get the hell out of here!"

Lute stood quietly and listened to the torrent of words spilling from her mouth.

"Calm down. There's a world of difference between city street gangs and a bunch of high school kids out celebrating a football victory. Of course I realize you didn't know that."

"You think I'm a fool!" She watched him move about the kitchen as if he lived here. He took a pan from the cabinet and milk from the refrigerator.

"You need something hot to drink. So do I."

"Then go home and get it," Nelda said in what she hoped was a nasty voice. "Your mother wouldn't approve of your being here."

"What's my mother got to do with it?" He spoke with his back to her.

"She's very concerned that I'll upset your orderly life. She said you'd come to sleep with me, but that was all. If you're hanging around for that, Lute, you might as well go, because I'm not sleeping with you...ever again! Go find Miss Home Ec—I'm sure she'll oblige you." All the resentment that had been bottled up inside her was pouring out. She wanted to pierce his calm shell, somehow find a way to make him suffer.

"The way you oblige Norris Smithfield?" He turned abruptly, and her bitter gaze locked with his while her mouth tightened with anger.

"Yes, if you must know!" she hissed, and the bleak look that crossed his face brought a pleased little flutter to her rapid heartbeat.

His eyes assessed her critically, moving, she knew, over the short curly hair to her tear-wet eyes and the lips that were trying so hard not to tremble. She did her best to return his gaze coolly, but she was very near the breaking point.

"Where's the chocolate?"

She looked at him as if he had lost his mind. Her face was tight with emotion and her eyes, though glazed with tears, looked defiantly into his.

"I don't want you here, Lute. This is my house, and I don't want you here." Her voice was savage, raw in her own ears.

He turned his back to her and began to open cabinet doors. He found the box of cocoa mix and set it on the counter along with two mugs.

"Don't make me lose my temper, Nelda," he said softly.

"Then don't make me lose mine. Now I'd appreciate it if you'd go. I can handle things from here on. I'm going to that lousy sheriff tomorrow to file a complaint. You know who those hoodlums were. You'll have to name them, or you'll be in contemp of court." She knew she was being unreasonable, but she couldn't seem to stop spewing her anger. "This is my home. I own it. I've . . . got a right to be here and not be bothered in the middle of the night." Her voice began to break. "You *never* had any respect for my feelings. You never even tried to understand how I felt about wanting to accomplish something on my own after Becky died," she blurted.

"You never understood my feelings about anything, either. Now shut up and drink this." He set the cup of warm chocolate down in front of her, picked up his own, and stood with his back to the counter.

She knew his intense gaze was focused on her face, but she refused to look at him. The smell of the chocolate was nauseating. She pressed one hand to her abdomen and willed her stomach to settle down. It would be the final humiliation if she had to throw up.

"If you're sure the boys were doing more than trespassing, if they threatened you or tried to break into the house, you should file a complaint. But you must be very sure before you make a charge that will stay on a boy's record for the rest of his life."

"Chauvinist!" She spat the word at him. "We must protect the boys! What about me? If you'd found them raping me, I suppose you'd have thought I lured them in here! That I was 'asking for it'."

"There are times when I'd like to slap you!"

"Why don't you? Are you afraid of the gun? Here it is!" She took it out of her pocket and slammed it down on the table.

Lute reached over and picked it up. "Do you know how to handle this thing?"

"You're damn right I do. I took a course in self-defense. A woman alone has to look after herself."

"Oh, I imagine you could have found any number of men to look after you." Before she could retort he asked, "Do you have a permit for this?"

"A New York state permit. I suppose *here* they don't give gun permits to women." She said it sarcastically and drew in her lower lip, her voice stiff with brittle cynicism.

"We're not as red-necked as all that." His voice was caustic, his lips tight in an obvious attempt at self-control.

Nelda tried to tense her body so it would stop trembling. Her eyes flicked restlessly, trying to avoid him, but his presence seemed to fill every corner of the room. *Damn you! Damn you! Get out of here so I can bawl!*

"Why didn't you call Norris tonight?"

She glanced at him. He was watching her with a taut expression. "He's in Chicago," she said simply.

"Too bad. It would have been a good excuse for him to stay the night."

"He doesn't need an excuse," she said rashly, looking up to meet angry blue eyes. His face was harsh and powerful, the jaw jutting in an obvious effort to control his temper. Nelda sucked in her breath and bent her head over her cup.

"Are you moving in with him?" The words sounded torn out of him.

"Why would I want to do that?" She enjoyed seeing him squirm for a change. But then, he probably didn't care whom she slept with. He just didn't like Norris.

"Why not? He hasn't had a live-in for a while."

"You don't know anything about him. Just because he's rich and free to do as he pleases, you and the rest of your narrow-minded friends would like to think him a cad, a debaucher of young women, the sexual sultan of north Iowa!" She knew her anger was making her defense of Norris too vehement, but she couldn't make herself stop.

"So it's like that, eh?"

"Like what, Mister know-it-all?"

"You're in love with him!"

Hysterical laughter bubbled up in her throat. She had finally touched a raw spot! She turned her face up to meet his accusing stare.

"I can't believe you! For over two months I've—" She started to deny that she was in love with Norris, then cut herself off. She was tired, and it was suddenly easier to let him think what he wanted to think.

"How long are you going to be here?" he asked quietly.

"I haven't decided. I may just stay and take up farming. What kind of lease do you hold on my land?" She paused, her mind racing. "Norris will furnish me with all the equipment I need." The reckless words were out of her mouth before she could stop them.

He was silent for so long that she looked up and surprised the grin on his face. It infuriated her.

"I suppose you think I don't have brains enough to farm . . . can beans, freeze corn, slop hogs, feed chickens, etcetera, etcetera." It was crazy, but she had no control over her own words. *Why am I saying these things? Why don't I shut up?*

The eyes that blazed into hers were astonishingly bright with anger. "If you think this is such a stupid place, why do you stay? I'm getting a bit tired of your derogatory references to this area. You haven't changed a bit. You're an A1 snob, Nelda, just like your mother. I can still hear her say, 'Oh, Nelda Elaine, he's just a farmer!' That's exactly what I am, what I always will be, what I'm proud of being." He seemed to abruptly check his hostility, then continued, "But what I am, and what I will be, has nothing to do with you." He looked as if he hated her. "Don't threaten me with taking up permanent residence here. You wouldn't last a season, with or without Smithfield's help."

"Get out!" she hissed, surprising herself that she could even speak.

"Hurts, doesn't it, to hear the truth about yourself," he jibed. He strode to the kitchen door.

Rage and frustration such as she had never known boiled up inside Nelda. She stood up abruptly, knocking her chair to the floor in the process. When he turned and grinned at her anger, she lost control. Her hand found the empty mug on the table, and she threw it at him. He dodged it, and it went crashing through the window of the kitchen door and thumped to the floor of the porch. The sound of the shattering glass was faint in her ears that seemed to be filled with a thunderous pounding.

Lute looked at her with astonishment. "What the hell . . . ?"

She stood wide-eyed with the back of her hand to her mouth while the realization of what she had done penetrated her scrambled mind. Then with a cry she ran out of the room and up the stairs to her bedroom, shut the door, and threw herself down on the bed, pulling the pillow over her head.

She cried bitterly. She had made an utter, complete fool of herself. She cried until her mind was numb with grief and remorse, knowing that she had destroyed any respect Lute might have had for her. She sank deeply into the pit of her misery, letting it close in over her.

When the storm of weeping passed, she took off her robe and crawled under the covers. She was shaking almost uncontrollably from taut nerves. She lay flat on her back, staring at nothing, as if her eyelids had been rendered powerless to close.

She could hear the sound of hammering down in the kitchen. Lute was still here. He was boarding up the window she had broken out of the door. Good of him, she thought absently. Why was he bothering? It wouldn't mean anything to him if she froze to death.

A feeling of desperate loneliness flooded her heart. Even her dog had deserted her to stay downstairs with Lute. She was wanted or needed by no one except the tiny life that grew inside her. She was worse than useless as far as Lute was concerned. They had needed each other when they were young and thought the whole world was against them, but now . . . Trying to keep the pain in her heart at bay, she decided that tomorrow she would call Marlene in Minneapolis and see if she knew of an apartment for rent. It was ridiculous to stay here any longer.

"Nelda. Are you all right?" Lute pushed open the bedroom door. Kelly trotted in and flopped down beside the bed.

"You're always asking me that. What do you care?" she responded dully.

"Don't be foolish. I asked, are you all right?"

"I heard you. I may be stupid, but I'm not deaf."

"Stop being childish, Nelda. I didn't realize you were so shaken by what happened." She didn't answer. "I had a piece of plywood in the truck. I nailed it over the broken glass in the door. It'll keep the cold out until you can get it fixed. Call the hardware store in the morning. They'll send someone out." He paused. "Nelda . . . did you hear me?" He came to the side of the bed. "Oh, Nelda . . . why is it always like this? We—"

"Get out," she interrupted. "I'm sorry I called you. I'm not your concern. I won't bother you again."

"It was no bother." He sat down on the edge of the

bed. "You don't look well. Have you been sick?"

"No. I'm not sick, I'm just not the robust type. You've got me confused with Miss Home Ec, the all-American girl. I'd never be able to lift hay bales and milk cans. I'm just not built that way."

Now it was his turn to be silent. She looked at him almost calmly in the dim light.

"Go home, Lute," she said softly. "I'm getting my act together, and I'll be out of your hair soon."

He got up and went to the door. "I left the pistol in the cabinet above the refrigerator." He waited, but when she didn't speak he went out the door and down the stairs. She heard him close the back door. Soon she heard the pickup driving down the lane toward the road.

He called about noon the next day.

"Hello, Nelda? This is Lute."

"I know who it is," she said tightly.

"Are you still upset?"

"What do you want, Lute?" she said sharply, trying to erect a barrier around her feelings.

"I've talked to the boys who were at your place last night. They want you to accept their apology. They won't trespass on your property again."

"That's good to hear."

"Well?"

"Well . . . what?"

"Do you accept their apology? Is this the end of it?"

"What did you think I'd do? Carry on a vendetta, put out a contract, notify my New York mafia friends?"

"You little—"

"Now, now! Remember, I'm just a good old country girl."

"Knock off the sarcasm. I'm in no mood for it. Did you get someone out there to fix that window?"

She couldn't take another moment of his solicitousness, knowing it had nothing to do with his heart and everything to do with his concern for some high-school boys' criminal records. He wasn't ever really being kind— he was just expecting her to always fail, always do the wrong thing.

"Goodbye, Lute," she whispered hoarsely.

She hung up the phone.

Soon thereafter the man from the hardware store in town came out and replaced the broken window pane. Nelda ordered a heavy bolt to be put on the inside of the porch door.

"Somebody try to break in, did they?" She said nothing, feeling slightly guilty for her silence. "Young scallywags out a roamin' 'round, too lazy to do a day's work," he continued undaunted. "You can't get a one of 'em to work for minimum wage. No siree! They got to get union pay, and if'n they don't get it, they don't lift a hand." The man talked nonstop. "These kids need the draft brought back, that's what they need. Get 'em in the army—that'd take the starch out of 'em."

Oh, no! He sounds just like my father did ten years ago, Nelda thought, and she tried to keep busy in another part of the house until he finished his work.

When he left she called Marlene and asked her help in finding an apartment, explaining simply that she wanted to move to Minneapolis as soon as possible.

"Give me a day or two to scout around, and I'll get back to you. Are you feeling well? You sound depressed."

"I'm going through a bout of morning sickness, but other than that I'm fine. I think I need to get settled so I can begin making some long-range plans."

"Then we'll get you settled—as close to me as possible."

"Thank you, Marlene. By the way, I haven't seen Norris for a while."

"He came to the Twin Cities yesterday, then went back to Chicago. He has a lot of corporate business to

attend to now. He really has very heavy responsibilities,"
she added almost shyly, her pride obvious in her voice.

"Are you sure this isn't going to be too much bother?
I could call a realtor."

"No! no! I'll love doing it. I'll call you in a day or
two. Take care."

After talking to Marlene, Nelda felt better. She called
Rhetta to lay the groundwork for leaving.

"Oh, no!" Rhetta said when she told her she had to
return to New York to work on a project for a favorite
client.

"It isn't forever," Nelda laughed. "I'm leaving a lot
of my things. I'll be back."

"You're not leaving before the Harvest Ball, are you?"
Rhetta wailed. "I'm planning on your helping with the
decorations."

"Oh, I'm not sure, Rhetta."

"When will you be sure?"

"In a day or two. But if I'm here, I'll help, how's
that?"

"It'll just have to do, I guess."

Marlene called two days later to tell her she had already found a dream of an apartment. It was small—
one bedroom, a combined kitchen and dining area—but
the living room was large and had floor-to-ceiling windows all along one wall. It was within walking distance
of a shopping center. "A rather long walk," Marlene
added ruefully.

"It sounds perfect. I'll have my car, but I'm going to
need exercise," Nelda assured her.

"There's a catch. It won't be ready for occupancy
until the first of the month. That's almost two weeks
away. Can you hold out until then? If not, come stay
with me. Or I'm sure you can use Norris's apartment if
you want more privacy. He may not come back to the
Cities for a while, but if he does, he won't mind staying
in a hotel."

"I can stay here until the first. Thank you, Marlene.
I'm so glad I met Norris—so glad I met you."

"Me too. I'm looking forward to having you near me.
If anything comes up and you want to come sooner, let
me know."

Staying at the farm another two weeks would mean
Thanksgiving alone in Grandma's house, where she had
observed it many times among family when she was a
child. But this would be her last Thanksgiving
alone. . . . Next year she would have the baby, and he
would be six months old. She automatically thought of
the baby as *he*. She started going over names for him in
her mind. Severt, after Grandpa. No, she didn't think
he'd like that name as he was growing up. Scott Edward
Hanson. She liked the sound of it, and he would have
Grandpa's initials. The thought suddenly struck her that
by next Christmas "Scotty" would be the same age as
Becky was when that mysterious crib death . . . She forcibly banished the thought from her mind.

The week before Thanksgiving she stopped working
at the library, returned the red pickup to the rental agency,
and brought the Oldsmobile home. She also had a long
meeting with Mr. Hutchinson, her attorney and farm
manager, and told him he was to make arrangements
immediately to sell the farm. She would make arrangements later, she told him, for her personal things to be
removed from the house. She ignored the questioning
look on his face and the gentle prodding for the reason
she had changed her mind after telling him numerous
times she would never sell the land that had been in her
family for generations.

When Rhetta called about helping with the decorations
for the Harvest Ball, Nelda begged off due to a cold. It
was not a contrived excuse. She hadn't felt well for
several days.

"You're off the hook, love. Get the sniffles cleared
up, because no way are you going to miss out on the big

bash. You're going with the right honorable veterinarian and his spouse, and I won't let you wiggle out of it."

"But, Rhetta, I don't want to go without an escort. If Norris gets back I'm sure he'll take me, but—"

"Baloney!" Rhetta interrupted. "There'll be dozens of men and women without escorts. In our town a woman would sit home all the time if she had to depend on a date. Think nothing of it, and plan on being at our place at about eight. Okay?"

Reluctantly Nelda agreed to go. It would be her last opportunity to see Lute. It was something she looked forward to and yet dreaded. She'd wear the heavy silk emerald green caftan. The color was a perfect foil for her light skin, dark hair and eyes, and the loose fit would conceal her thickening waistline. The one nagging concern she had about going was having to see Lute with Janythe Graham.

Nelda stood in front of the cheval glass and studied herself critically. The makeup she had applied to the dark circles beneath her eyes had done it's job, but even knowing that she looked her best did nothing to put her into a partying mood. She sprayed perfume from an atomizer and watched the fragrant mist settle on the soft curls surrounding her face. Involuntarily her heart leaped at the thought of seeing Lute and perhaps dancing with him for the last time.

At a quarter to eight she pulled on her snow boots, put on her heavy coat, and carefully pulled the hood up over her hair. Nervous as a schoolgirl off to her first prom, she picked up her small purse and slender-heeled shoes and went out to the garage. The night was cold and still. She pumped the accelerator several times before she tried to start her car. When she finally turned the key nothing happened. Absolutely nothing. She tried the lights. Again nothing. She breathed deeply, trying to calm her nerves so she could think rationally. The battery

in the car was dead. Good! The perfect excuse not to go
to the Harvest Ball.

Back in the house she dialed Rhetta's number.

"Hi. Guess what? My car's battery is dead, so I won't
be joining you tonight. Have a gorgeous time, and I'll
call you tomorrow to hear all about it—that is, if your
head will allow you to talk on the phone." Nelda even
managed a small laugh.

"Hold it!" Rhetta's voice was insistent. "Just hold it!
There'll be someone there for you in ten minutes. I'll
send Gary or someone."

"No, Rhetta. I've already undressed." It was a fib that
came easily to her lips.

"Ten minutes. 'Bye." The phone went dead.

"Oh, damn!"

When she saw headlights coming up the lane, she
pulled up the hood on her coat, picked up her shoes and
purse, and stepped out into the crisp cold. The car swung
toward and then away from her, momentarily blinding
her with its highbeams, and then backed up so the passenger door was toward her. The door opened, and the
interior light came on. Nelda abruptly recognized the
car—and the driver. Lute sat behind the wheel. She was
so startled she just stood and stared. Lute, in a dark suit
and topcoat, leather gloves on his hands that gripped the
wheel, and a grim look on his face, turned to face her.

Oh, no! Nelda thought. What now?

"Get in. The car's warm, but it won't be if you stand
there much longer with the door open."

Almost mindless, Nelda got in and shut the door.

Chapter
9

THE CLOSING OF the car door brought blessed darkness, but almost immediately the scent of peppery, male cologne assaulted her nostrils, sending explosive quivers through her. She adjusted her coat, buying time and courage. Nothing could have been harder than being with Lute so unexpectedly, yet her heart sang and her pulses drummed with excitement. I'll miss him desperately for the rest of my life, she thought, but I'll store up all these little last-minute images of him to carry in my mind.

The car left the gravel road and pulled out onto the highway. The silence was heavy. Not a word had passed between them since Lute had told her so bluntly to get into the car. Nelda felt as if the two of them were involved in some last, elaborate game; her purpose being to behave normally, and his to endure her presence with a minimum of civility.

"Sorry to put you to this bother. Rhetta said Gary would come for me," she offered in the way of apology.

"No bother. I was coming past your place anyway. What's wrong with your car?"

She met his glance with a pretense of calm. "Battery. I'll have someone out tomorrow."

"Tomorrow is Thanksgiving."

"Oh. That's right, it is. Friday then."

There was another long, tense silence. Nelda stared at the ribbon of highway unwinding before them, wondering how she was going to bear seeing him with Janythe Graham.

"Rhetta tells me you're leaving soon. You stuck it out longer than I thought you would." He changed gears violently, and the car shuddered.

"What do you mean by that?" She knew, but she still had to challenge him.

"You know what I mean." He glanced at her quickly and back to the road.

"Yes, I guess I do," she murmured, watching his dark profile.

A car swept down the road toward them, the headlights flashing briefly over his face. His lips were pressed tightly together, and his brows were beetled into a frown. His silence made her tense, and she began to shiver.

"Cold?" he asked instantly.

"A little."

He switched the heater control, sending a waft of warm air over her legs. "Is that better?"

"Much," she said, cuddling down in pretended comfort. "This is a nice car. I'm so used to seeing you in a pickup that . . ." Her voice trailed away. She didn't know how to finish what she'd started.

"Farmers nowadays can afford a few luxuries. They send their kids to college, take winter trips to Hawaii or Las Vegas occasionally, and, in my case, have a sporty car." He was keeping his voice firmly under control, allowing only a hint of sarcasm to surface.

"I know that," she said sharply. "I've enjoyed the income from Grandpa's farm for almost a year now."

"That's right, you have. The money is good, but the life-style stinks, right?" he said in clipped tones, which no longer hid from her his feelings of contempt.

Nelda felt her skin flushing, and she looked away from him. Let him think what he wants to think, she thought bitterly. Lute slowed the car as he turned up the drive toward the house and circled to park so she wouldn't have to wade through snow to get to the door. As soon as he braked to a stop she fumbled for the door handle and pressed it, but it was locked. Lute cut the motor and lights, then turned in the seat to look at her.

After a brief silence he said flatly, "You're not coming back."

"No," she said, deciding to make an honest break.

"When are you going?" he asked without emotion.

She tried for lightness in her voice. "I haven't decided, but soon. I've got a wonderful opportunity to decorate an advertising studio. If I can come up with something spectacular, I'll truly be set in my career. The clients will be breaking down the door to get to me."

"And that's important to you?"

"Sure. It's what I trained for," she said, not meeting his eyes.

"Smithfield would fit into your life perfectly, wouldn't he?" The question was brutally sharp.

"Well . . . I guess so."

"No guess about it. You two zeroed in on each other like homing pigeons!" The vehemence in his voice was frightening.

She tried the door handle again. It still refused to give.

"Thank you for picking me up. I'm sure you want to get going and pick up your date." Nelda felt her composure slipping through her fingers, but she also felt envy for the woman who would be by his side all evening.

"You're my date," he said simply.

She turned, surprised by his words, and found he had leaned closer to her, his eyes finding hers and holding them.

"What do you mean?" she choked.

"Just what I said." He seemed to jerk the words through tight lips. "We're a twosome, a couple, a duet . . . a pair for the evening, anyway."

Nelda drew back. He was too close! She could see the color of his eyes and smell the freshness of his breath. Irrational anger bubbled up inside her.

"I don't recall making a date with you. Now, let me out of this damn car."

"Why are you so riled?"

"I'm not riled, damnit! Well, yes, I am. You make me so mad I don't know what I'm thinking, much less what I'm saying. You take a lot of things for granted, Lute. Didn't it occur to you to call and ask me to go out with you this evening?" She took a deep breath. "It's the same old story . . . you keep everything bottled up inside you. I never knew what you were thinking, or feeling, or wanting."

"You know what I want." He was grinning now.

"You're being obnoxious! I'm not talking about physical want. I'm talking about—"

"I know what you're talking about, but I'm talking about the one line of communication we had that was good right up to the very last—and still good after all this time. Your tight little body fits into all the hollows of mine like it was made to order." His voice lowered into raspiness. "I'm going to kiss you, Nelda Elaine. What are you going to do about it?"

She looked at him through her lashes and knew she wasn't going to do a thing. She wanted him to kiss her, hold her, make her blood rush around her body, make a thousand little memories for her to tuck away and bring out again and again in her lonely future. She turned her eyes away, afraid he would read her thoughts.

Lute reached out to cradle the nape of her neck and pull her head toward him. His face was grave, and his eyes held a tenderness she didn't expect. Nelda felt the strength drain out of her, leaving her limp in his grasp.

"You'll smear my makeup," she said feebly.

"You don't need makeup. Never did."

"Rhetta will be wondering—"

"To hell with Rhetta."

"I don't want you to kiss me."

"Liar."

"I'm not."

"I could always tell when you were lying."

"I don't lie."

"You do. Now hush."

Nelda gazed back into his eyes, so astonishingly blue and luminous in the dim light. She clamped her mouth shut and tried to look away from him, but in the closeness of the small car, and with his hand holding her still, there was nowhere else to look. He not only filled her eyes, but her thoughts, her mind.

Suddenly his eyes were twinkling. He was trying to keep his mouth from spreading into a wide grin, and his face was coming closer to hers.

"That mouth of yours always tells me what you're thinking. Right now your lips are pressed together—you're being stubborn; when I kiss you they'll soften, because you like my kissing you. You draw your bottom lip between your teeth when you're puzzled and uncertain, and the corners of your mouth lift when you want to laugh but are trying not to. You get mad fast, but you get over it fast, too. Remember when you bit me?" He drew in a quivering breath. "As soon as your teeth let go of my lip you were crying and kissing it. You were awfully sweet in those days."

That reminder of the past tore at her heart. "Those days are over," she whispered.

"Yes." He said it softly and took her chin tightly in his hand. She attempted to twist away from him, but he held her firmly and kissed her gently on the mouth. She tried to close her heart against the thrill of his lips, the soft brush of his mustache, and the gentle look in his eyes. "The first time I kissed you was on a cold night after the last football game of the season. We were sitting in the pickup with a blanket over our legs because I didn't have enough gas to keep the engine running."

"Why are you bringing that up now?" Her heart was haunted and dark with despair, and she tried to push him away.

"I don't know. I guess you never really forget your first love." With her hand in the powerful grip of his two hands, he slowly lowered his lips to hers and kissed her with slow deliberation, his lips playing, coaxing. Never had she had to fight so hard not to surrender completely, to cling to him and beg him to stay with her forever, tell him that a part of him would be with her always. Was he playing with her? With blinding clarity the truth hit her: he knew his power over her!

"Lute, no!" She pulled back, and he let her go. "Rhetta will be wondering what in the world we're doing."

"Okay. I wouldn't want Rhetta to get the idea that I'm out here kissing my ex-wife. It could ruin my image of love 'em and leave 'em." The tender look was gone from his eyes, and his words were fringed with sarcasm.

"What you're really afraid of is that Miss Home Ec will find out." Her sarcasm matched his.

"You're right," he said caustically. "I've got to have someone to fill in when you leave."

She balled a fist, wishing she had the nerve to swing it into his face.

He reached across her and released the door. The interior light came on, and Nelda collected her shoes and purse. Without looking at him she got out of the car. By the time she reached the porch he was beside her, his hand on her elbow. She wanted to jerk away, but the thoughts rushed in like ocean waves—last kiss . . . last touch. . . .

Rhetta threw open the door. "Well, you two. I was about to call out the emergency squad. I thought you'd slid into a ditch somewhere."

"Nothing as exciting as that," Nelda said with forced lightness in her voice. She glanced at Lute. He was so

handsome standing there, his dark suit dramatically setting off his blond hair, that she could scarcely tear her
eyes away from him.

"Come have a drink. Gary is late, as usual. Do you
like my dress?" She whirled. "I added the rose sash like
you suggested, Nelda. I think it did wonders for it. Oh
here, give me your coat. Better yet, you take it, Lute.
Oh dear! Isn't it awful to have to wear snow boots with
an evening dress?" Rhetta's eyes ping-ponged continu-
ously between Nelda and Lute. "Your dress is lovely!
That color is great for you. Don't you think so, Lute?"

"Great," Lute said softly, his eyes on Nelda's burning
cheeks.

Nelda rushed into speech. "If we're going to be here
a while I'll take off my boots."

"No, leave them on. Gary's getting dressed, and if
he knows we're having a drink he'll hurry." Rhetta was
relaxed and smiling. "What'll you have, Lute? Fix something for yourself and Nelda, and I'll dash up and make
sure Gary gets into the right clothes. I'll be surprised if
he finds everything, even though I've laid it out on the
bed for him."

Nelda tried to throw off the suspicion that had begun
to grow on her little by little: Rhetta was contriving to
throw her and Lute together. She was leaving them alone,
and there had been a vivid sparkle in her eyes, as though
she were feeling triumphant.

The intense silence that followed Rhetta's departure
seemed to press in on her. Her face felt stiff, her body
devoid of the strength necessary to turn and face Lute.

"What will you have, Nelda? Gary keeps a well-stocked
liquor cabinet." Lute's voice floated across the room,
and she turned to look at his back.

"Nothing, thank you."

"You drank the night you were here with Smithfield,"
he said, the words dripping venom.

"I wasn't here with Norris. I just met him here." She looked at the amount of whiskey he'd poured into a glass, and she closed her eyes in misery. When she opened them he had started across the room toward her.

"You look as though you could use a drink. Are you sure you're well?" He had added soda to the whiskey.

"Thanks a lot! Every woman loves to hear she looks like death warmed over when she's dressed for a party." She held the drink, knowing she couldn't possibly get a swallow down her tight throat.

"Fishing for a compliment? You know you're a beautiful woman. You don't need to be told."

"Oh, shut up, Lute," she said crossly. "I'm beginning to wish I'd stayed at home with a good book."

"Don't worry, the party will liven you up. You just might be the belle of the ball."

"Here we are!" Rhetta announced. "Isn't he gorgeous?" She beamed at Gary, who on cue tucked his thumbs into the lapels of his jacket and pivoted like a model.

"I hear they're looking for male strippers over at the Velvet Touch, Gary. Maybe you could get a job there," Lute said drily.

"Jealous, m'lad. That's what's wrong with you. You're jealous of my good looks and my charm, but I forgive you. Let's be off." He grabbed Rhetta and whirled her around. "I want to dance with my beautiful wife."

Nelda felt a stab of envy, and before she could stop them her eyes flew to Lute. She could hear some strange sounds from the past . . . a band at a prom and Lute saying over the music, *If anyone asks you to dance, I'll punch him in the nose*. How had their love slipped away? Could she have held it if she had come back sooner—or had it died the moment she left him?

* * *

The evening was already a total disaster as far as Nelda was concerned. Her strained nerves were near the breaking point by the time they reached the hall where the dance was being held.

Their arrival caused a stir in the small, already crowded ballroom. Faces turned, voices dropped to whispers, and Nelda knew from the curious glances she was getting that people were wondering who was with Lute Hanson. Then realization...she was the woman from New York living on the Severt Hansen farm. Lute appeared unperturbed by the stares. He seemed to know everybody.

Nelda looked around, recognized a few people she had met through her work at the library, smiled her greetings, and clutched her small jeweled purse as though it were a talisman. Rhetta beckoned, and the two of them went to the ladies' room to check their appearance and makeup.

As though reading her thoughts, Rhetta asked, "You're not nervous about being here with Lute?"

"Well...yes, I am," Nelda said unsteadily. "I wish you hadn't sent him for me, Rhetta. I'm sure he had a date."

"No, he didn't. He was coming with Gary and me. I don't think he's seeing anyone now," she continued, suggestion blatant in her voice.

Nelda added a final touch of lipgloss with a calmness of manner she didn't feel and swung around to face Rhetta. "I'll be leaving soon, and I don't want any entanglements. Miss Home Ec is welcome to him."

Rhetta looked at her steadily, and Nelda knew she was taking in her quivering lower lip, the eyes that looked away, the hands that shook when she returned the lipstick to her purse.

"I don't believe that for a minute. But never mind, let's get back to the party."

Lute was in an animated group near the front door. Nelda slipped past and edged her way to the other side of the room, where she found a chair beside a potted plant. She was chilled with nerves and wished fervently that the evening was already over. She watched Rhetta and Gary, their bodies locked tightly together from shoulder to thigh, dancing a slow waltz.

A sudden fear almost bowled her over. I've got to get out of here, she thought frantically. What if I have to dance with Lute? He'll know I'm pregnant! Why didn't I think of that? My waist is thicker, my breasts fuller. He'll notice, I know he will!

As if on cue, a deep voice spoke from beside her, "Nelda."

She froze, her heart turning to ice. She didn't need to see the face; the voice could belong to only one man in the world. The sound of music, the revelry in the background all receded to a distant murmur in her ears. There was only the tall form beside her, the blond head bending to hers, and the soft voice saying, "Dance with me, Nelda."

"I can't!" she blurted. "I...don't feel well. I'd like to sit quietly for a while," she continued weakly.

Lute drew up a chair and sat down close beside her. "I thought something was wrong with you. You're sick! What's the matter? Do you have a temperature?" The concern in his voice brought a painful ache to her chest, and she had to force back tears.

"I may have a little fever, but I'll be all right."

"Do you want to go home?"

"No. I'm all right." Her voice stuck in her throat, and she dared not look at him. She kept her face averted. I can't let him take me home and run the risk of giving in to temptation and letting him spend the night. That would be disastrous! "I'll be all right," she repeated. That's the third time I've said that, she thought crazily. "Go on and dance, Lute. You always loved to dance."

"What's the matter?" he asked quietly.

"Flu, I guess." She wanted to scream, *I'm pregnant,*

I've got a perfect right to not feel well!

"You shouldn't have come," he observed.

"Try telling that to Rhetta once she's made up her mind."

"You could have told *me*." His soft, concerned voice threatened what remained of her self-control.

She clenched her hands so tightly the nails bit into the palms, but she felt no pain. Every particle of sensation was concentrated on keeping the tears from her eyes. She knew people were looking at her and Lute, wondering why they were sitting there, not dancing. Will this evening never end, she thought deperately.

The music stopped, and Rhetta and Gary approached them. "Why aren't you two dancing?"

"Nelda doesn't feel well, Rhetta. She shouldn't have come." Lute stood up and reached out his hand as if to pull Nelda to her feet.

"You can dance with my wife this once, Lute. I'll put it on your next bill. I'll sit with Nelda." Gary moved around and sat down in the chair Lute vacated.

Rhetta took Lute's arm, and they moved away. Nelda watched them until they were lost in the crowd of dancers.

"I hate to desert you, Gary, but I think I'll go to the ladies' room." Nelda got unsteadily to her feet.

"It's a bloody shame you're under the weather, love. Is there anything I can do?"

"I'll be fine. Guard the chairs, will you? It looks as if they're going to get scarce. I'll take a couple of aspirin."

Without any conscious notion of what she was going to do, Nelda hurried around the throng of dancers and headed toward the lobby. Did this town have a taxi? She couldn't remember having seen one. She'd get her coat and boots and at least get out the door while Lute was dancing with Rhetta.

A cheery voice interrupted her flight. "There you are.

I thought I might find you here."

Nelda jerked to a stop. Norris stood grinning at her. Her relief was more than she could bear, and the tears started running down her cheeks. She clutched his arm.

"Help me get out of here!" Her voice cracked with the effort to say the words.

The smile abruptly left Norris's face. "Sure, honey. Where's your coat?"

"It's there in the racks. I'll get it." Almost frantic in her haste, she found her coat and boots and returned to find Norris putting on his coat.

Minutes later they were in his car, and she was sobbing helplessly.

"I don't know what I would have done if you hadn't been there. I was going to go out and try to find someone. I had to get out of there. I was crazy to come in the first place, but Rhetta was so insistent. I thought it would be easier to come than to make excuses."

Norris pushed a handkerchief into her groping fingers. "I called the house, and when there was no answer I figured Rhetta had dragged you to this thing. I didn't dare go to the Cities tomorrow without taking a report to Marlene."

"Rhetta sent Lute to get me, and I knew if I danced with him he'd know I was pregnant." Nelda was completely absorbed in her misery. "I was out of my mind to get myself into this situation!"

Nelda dried her tears while Norris stopped the car at a public telephone booth, called the hall, and had Rhetta paged. He explained that Nelda was with him, so there was no need to worry.

"Rhetta was none too pleased," he said when he returned to the car. "Lute will be furious. I know I would be if someone ran off with my date."

"He won't mind. He was a victim of Rhetta's persuasion, too."

"I hate to take you home and leave you alone," Norris

said as he eased the car off the highway and onto the snowpacked gravel road. "But I have a plane waiting for me at the airport. I just stopped over for an hour or so."

"Are you spending Thanksgiving with Marlene?"

"Yes, I am. Why don't you come along? Marlene would love to see you."

"It's sweet of you to ask, but no thanks. I'll be leaving in three days, and I've got to sort and pack what I want sent to me. I've also got to have something done with my car. I wish tomorrow wasn't Thanksgiving so I could get someone out to fix it."

"That's no problem," he assured her.

Kelly was waiting for them beside the kitchen door. He stretched lazily, and Nelda felt a wave of relief to be back in the safety of the farmhouse. She smiled at Norris, not caring that her mascara was smeared from her bout of tears.

"You and Marlene are so lucky to have each other. Why do you hide the real you behind that playboy image?"

"It's easier to be what people expect you to be than what you are. If you're rich and unmarried and flit around the country—even if your trips are business related—you get the reputation of being a pleasure seeker. I know what I am, the woman I love knows what I am, so to hell with what everyone else thinks. Now . . . let me get to the phone so we can get someone out here in the morning to put a new battery in your car."

Nelda supplied the make and the model of the car, and after a few minutes on the phone arrangements were made for a wrecker to come out first thing in the morning and give the car a complete check.

"Can I ask one more favor of you, Norris?"

"Of course you can, Chicken Little. Anything."

"After I leave here, will you arrange to have my things sent to me? I don't want anyone to know I'm in the Twin Cities. It's very important to me to lose myself for a while."

"Are you sure you want to do this, honey? Lute's a hell of a nice fellow, although he's had a complete personality change since you've been here. I'm sure he still loves you. Don't you think he's entitled to know you're having his child?"

"He mustn't know! It isn't a question of whether he's entitled to know or not. I don't want him to know. When I'm gone he can marry one of his . . . native lady friends and forget all about me." Tears filled her eyes, and she blinked rapidly.

Norris rubbed his knuckles across her cheek. "You love him desperately, don't you, Chicken Little? We'll play it the way you want it, but if you change your mind, he won't be far away."

"I won't change my mind. He was forced to marry me once before because I was pregnant, and I'm sure he would do so again. You're wrong, Norris, about his feelings for me. He never made any attempt to get in touch with me during the years we were apart. He thinks I'm dedicated to my career and completely unsuitable for his kind of life. He's old fashioned where women are concerned. He'd never allow his wife an interest outside the farm, and I'm not sure I'd be able to handle that."

"He's a fool!" Norris snorted. "But then, that's his problem."

"Tell Marlene I'll be up on Monday, and take her this kiss." She planted a gentle kiss on his cheek.

He grinned roguishly. "That was certainly prudish! Can't you do any better than that?"

Nelda laughed and poked at his chest with her index finger. "Knock it off! You forget that I'm one of the privileged few who know the real you."

She stood beside the kitchen window and waved as he drove out of the yard. He answered with a toot of the horn.

Chapter

10

ONCE IN HER bedroom Nelda slipped out of the caftan and removed her underwear. She stood before the long mirror and studied her naked body. She was not happy with what she saw. Her arms and legs were thinner, and her collarbone protruded prominently. She had hard, dark shadows beneath her eyes, her cheekbones stood out as if she was half starved. Grimacing in distaste she turned away. She reminded herself of pictures she had seen of hungry children with bloated stomachs and large, hopeless eyes. I've got to eat more, she thought. This can't be good for the baby.

After a warm bath she fixed herself a cup of hot chocolate and a peanut butter and jelly sandwich and carried it back upstairs to the bedroom. The aftermath of her ordeal had left her exhausted. She crawled wearily into bed and nibbled on the sandwich.

When the harsh ringing of the telephone broke the stillness, she thought her heart skipped a beat. Mesmerized by the sound, she sat upright and stared at the instrument. Lute? It couldn't be. The dance wouldn't be over for another couple of hours. Maybe it was Rhetta, or Norris saying his take-off was delayed. She wasn't aware she was counting the rings, but on the fourth one she picked up the phone and held it a moment before she spoke.

"Hello," she whispered through stiff lips.

"Nelda! Are you all right?" It was Lute's voice, and there was exasperation in his tone.

"Yes. I'm...all right."

"What took you so long to answer the phone?"

"It only rang four times, Lute."

"Is Smithfield still there?" he demanded.

"No."

"Why did you leave like that? I offered to take you home. Did you know he was coming and wait for him?"

"I didn't know he was going to be there, and if I did it would be no business of yours. I wasn't your date. Rhetta shoved me at you, and we both know it. Now if you don't mind, I'm very tired."

"Don't hang up, Nelda. Have you been to a doctor lately? You don't look well. You've lost weight."

"The very words every girl longs to hear." Her voice had regained a crisp decisiveness.

"I don't need any of your cute answers, Nelda."

"And I don't need your interference, Lute."

"Why is it that we can't carry on a decent conversation? Every time I see you, you seem to get bitchier."

"Please notice that I haven't been seeking you out." Her voice was low, but she managed to keep it steady.

"You did one time."

"And was insulted for it!" Even as she said the words she knew they were unreasonable.

"I won't dignify that statement with an answer. What are you doing for dinner tomorrow?"

"I'll be eating a TV dinner and crying my eyes out because I'm not in the bosom of a large happy family eating turkey and dressing. Is that what you want to hear? If not, how's this—I'm thrilled to death to be eating alone, with no one to tell me how rotten I look and how bitchy I am!"

"How about coming to my place?" he asked calmly.

"No!" she exploded.

"How would it be if I brought something over there?" he continued sweetly.

"No. I'll be sleeping late, and I'm in no mood for

company." *Why are you being like this now, Lute,* her mind cried. *Why not when I first came back?*

"What you mean is, you don't feel like cooking. You won't have to, I will."

"No, Lute. I thank you for your concern, but I've been on my own for a good long while now. I'm quite capable of taking care of myself. I probably won't see you again before I leave, so goodbye. I'll always wish you the best." She hung up quickly before her voice could betray her. She kept her hand on the receiver, half expecting him to ring back, but he didn't. She lay back on the bed and let the tears fill her eyes.

At seven-thirty in the morning Kelly began to bark, alerting Nelda that someone was there. She got out of bed with a pounding headache—the result of last night's emotional upheaval, she realized—and went downstairs. A large wrecker had pulled up behind the car and was pulling it out of the garage. Two men were with it. She fastened Kelly to the end of his rope and let him out the door, then hurried to the bathroom and leaned her head over the commode.

Her head was pounding like it was caught in a vise, and her stomach was convulsing with dry heaves. She leaned weakly against the wall and wiped the perspiration from her face. When she thought she could make it, she stumbled back into the kitchen and rummaged in the cabinet for a handful of soda crackers. They helped sometimes, and she prayed they would now. She wanted to go back to bed, but she'd have to pay the men for the work on the car.

The crackers and a cup of tea settled her stomach, but her head continued to throb as if inspired to do so. She knew she looked less than presentable when she answered the knock on the door, but she was beyond caring.

"We need the car keys, ma'am, to check the new battery."

"Will you put the car back in the garage when you

finish?" she asked while she was fishing for the keys in her purse.

"Sure thing."

"If you'll give me the bill, I'll write you a check."

"Mr. Smithfield said to put it on his account." The man grinned sheepishly. "He runs a big account with us, ma'am, or we wouldn't have come out on Thanksgiving."

"I appreciate your coming. I'll settle with him."

After the men left Nelda took off her robe and settled down on the living room couch with a blanket and pillow. She hadn't felt this rotten in a long time. The next time she got up she would take her temperature, she promised herself. She dozed, woke, and dozed again.

Kelly was running through the house barking. It was a nightmare, of course. No, it was reality. Someone was at the door. Nelda struggled to awaken like a swimmer fighting to surface. When she stood and walked to the kitchen, her limbs were like lead. Shock gripped her throat when she saw Lute's face at the kitchen door. For a few seconds she stood as though turned to stone. Then, holding her flannel gown up so she could walk barefoot across the kitchen floor, she unlocked the door, immediately fleeing back to the couch in the living room.

"What do you want?" she called over her shoulder.

"Has Kelly been out?"

"Yes, but put him out again if he wants to go."

Nelda's eyes frantically swept the room for signs of the baby. Thank heavens she'd put away the books and the knitting; there was nothing visible to give away her secret.

Lute let Kelly out and then made several trips into the kitchen. Nelda couldn't see what he was doing from where she lay trembling on the couch, and she waited anxiously for him to come to the living room door.

"I knew you were sick." He stood leaning against the doorjamb. He was wearing jeans and a heavy knit pull-over sweater. "Have you taken your temperature?"

"No."

He shook his head and turned. She could hear his steps going toward the bathroom. He returned with the thermometer in his hand. "Open up," he said, and he poked it beneath her tongue. He stood looking down at her.

He looked so unnervingly attractive she had to admit to herself that if she didn't have a temperature now, she would have one soon. His lean brown face gleamed with a freshly shaven look, and his hair looked clean and shining. When her eyes lifted to him, his voice held teasing laughter.

"You look anything but the self-sufficient, sophisticated Ms. Hanson now. You look like a poor little pussycat dragged in out of the rain."

She reached to take the thermometer from her mouth so she could retort, but he grabbed her hand.

"Now, now. You'll have equal time later." He laughed deeply in his throat, and she glared up at him. He crouched down on his heels beside the couch, his palm cupping her chin so she couldn't open her mouth, and grinned at her. His face was so close she could see the small lines fan out from his eyes, the gold tips on the ends of his lashes, and her own reflection in his laughing eyes. "Bothers you, doesn't it? For once I have the advantage. You've got to lie there and listen to what I've got to say. No, keep quiet," he ordered when she made a throaty noise. "Mom made Thanksgiving dinner and put it in the freezer before she went south for the winter. I've brought it along. I'll thaw the turkey and dressing in the microwave, then put them in the oven to finish roasting." He picked up her wrist and circled it with his thumb and forefinger. He didn't say a word, but his eyes told her he was aware of her recent weight loss.

"There's giblet gravy, sweet potatoes, and pumpkin pie. Doesn't that whet your appetite?" He took the glass cylinder from her mouth and walked to the window. "Hmmmm, you do have a fever."

"How much?"

"Enough that you'll spend the day right there."

"How much, Lute?"

"Three degrees. I'll get a couple of aspirin, and we'll take it again later." One blond brow arched. "Aren't you glad I came over?"

"I'd have managed," she said ungraciously.

"That's gratitude for you!" He crossed the room to her and flipped the blanket off her feet. One large hand grasped a foot. "Your feet are warm. Why are you shaking?" He tucked her feet back under the warm gown and covered her with the blanket. "You're angry because I'm here, but you'll get over it when you smell the turkey and dressing." He tossed the words pleasantly over his shoulder and disappeared into the kitchen.

I've got to get myself together, Nelda thought desperately. I can't let him see how much I love him and how happy I am that he's here. In this mood he's almost...irresistible! He was lonely, she reasoned silently. He didn't want to spend the holiday alone. But Miss Home Ec would have shared it with him. Maybe he'd failed to ask her in time, and she'd gone out of town to be with her folks. Stop thinking and enjoy being with him, her heart told her, but her head argued. Her head said *it will be hell when you leave him after this,* but her heart said *it will be hell anyway.*

"Don't go to sleep before you take these." Lute's arm slipped beneath her shoulders and lifted her. She put the tablets in her mouth, and he held the glass of water to her lips. "Don't you think I'd make a good nurse? I've been practicing on the cows and the pigs. I've even delivered a litter of pups."

Nelda gulped. "Thanks! I'm flattered at the comparison!"

He laughed. "No comparison. I just want to assure

you that you're in experienced hands."

"That will be a comfort when the hearse comes to take me away."

"You won't shake my confidence with remarks like that." He tucked the blanket around her shoulders. "Do you want to watch Macy's Thanksgiving Day parade?"

"No. I'm not much of a television fan."

"You mean to say you don't watch 'Life of Love' or 'The Revolving World'?"

"I think you mean 'Love of Life' and 'As the World Turns,' but no, I don't watch them. I watch the news, a few old movies, and an occasional game."

"Then you should enjoy the football game this afternoon."

Lute's manner was easy, and a roguish light entered his eyes when he teased her. But on close inspection he looked tired. The smooth skin over his cheeks and jaw was tight and drawn, and the jeans that had fit him like a second skin in the late summer no longer did so. There was something different about him that frightened her a little.

"I do like football," she murmured.

"I remember," he said. "Now go back to sleep. I've got to let that pesky dog back in."

Nelda lay relaxed and content. She had to admit she enjoyed being pampered, especially by Lute. She stopped trying to understand his strange behavior and gave herself up to listening to him moving about the kitchen and talking to Kelly. How could he possibly think she could sleep knowing he was here, she wondered, and it was her last coherent thought before she dozed off.

The delicious smell of food cooking woke her. She lay with her eyes closed for a long moment, then opened them slowly. Lute was sitting in the big chair, his legs stretched out in front of him and his blond head resting on the back cushion. Kelly was standing with his head resting on Lute's thigh, and Lute's fingers were lost in the tangle of long red hair about the dog's ears. It was a picture she would carry in her heart forever. Lute turned his head, and their eyes met and held. A slow smile curved beneath the blond hair on his lip.

"It's about time you woke up. Do you feel better? I think I should take your temperature again before we eat." Kelly followed along behind him when he left the room and was still trailing him when he returned.

"I may sue you for alienation of affection. I thought I had a one-person dog." That was all she had time to say before the cold thermometer was popped into her mouth.

"He likes me. That's one smart dog."

Unable to talk, Nelda rolled her eyes to the ceiling in mock disgust. Lute laughed softly and went back to the kitchen. She watched him leave, her heart thumping up a storm. He'd removed his boots and was in his socks, heavy grey wool with blue toes and heels. He'd also taken off the heavy sweater, and the tan body-shirt he wore hugged his broad shoulders and tucked neatly into the waistband of his jeans. He was making himself at home, she thought with a pang. It was almost as if they lived here together.

She was trying to find the reading on the thermometer when he came up beside her and took it from her hand. He moved to the window.

"Are you sure you didn't shake it down?" he asked, squinting. "It's down a degree and a half."

"I didn't shake it down," she said quickly, and relief made her smile broadly.

"Okay. I'll take it again later. Dinner is ready. Do you want to go to the bathroom before we eat?" he asked with easy familiarity. "I went upstairs while you were sleeping and got your robe and slippers. I also brought down a cup of cold chocolate and a sandwich that looked like a mouse had nibbled on it," he said accusingly.

Nelda swung her legs off the couch and reached for

her slippers, but Lute evaded her hand, bent down, and slipped them over her toes. Her eyes lingered on the top of his blond head, and she found it hard to believe that he was really here. He pulled her to her feet and helped her into her robe while she stood like an obedient child, thanking God she had bought the bulky, loose-fitting, Mother Hubbard gown and robe.

"You're such a little thing." His eyes slid over her slowly, and he raised a finger to her cheek, gently caressing. "Little, but mighty." His voice was deep and husky with emotion.

Taken completely by surprise by this gentleness he'd shown so sporadically since her return, she moved abruptly away from him. But he took her arm and walked with her to the bathroom door, gave her a gentle shove into the room, and pulled the door closed firmly behind her.

Nelda stood inside the door, her hands tightly fisted at her side, her body rigid. I must be crazy, she thought wildly. I shouldn't have let him in. You fool, Nelda, you fool! You love his touch, you'd give your soul to melt in his arms! You could do it, her heart said. All you'd have to do is let him hold you and run his hands down your body. He'd haul you off to the minister tomorrow. But then what? He'd resent you for forcing him into an "unsuitable match," her common sense told her. He'd probably retreat back into the shell he was in when you left him. And how would he feel about having another child? What to do? Nothing, her heart dictated. Go with the tide, enjoy today. Tomorrow you can vanish from his life.

She looked at her reflection in the mirror. Hardly a woman a man could feel romantic about, she thought drily. Her face was pinched, her eyes dull, and her hair tumbled and ragged. She washed her face and hands and ran the comb through her hair. She considered adding a touch of lipstick but decided against it; he'd guess she had tried to look good for him.

He was taking a pan from the oven when she came out of the bathroom. One half of a small turkey lay in a nest of moist dressing.

"Get back on the couch. We're going to eat on TV trays."

"I can help," she offered weakly.

"And spoil my fun? Go get settled, and I'll bring you your plate."

Feeling useless but loving it, Nelda went back to the couch. Lute had set up the trays with napkins and silverware. The plate of food he brought to her looked delicious. He had arranged thin slices of white meat on a mound of dressing and topped it with giblet gravy. Sweet potatoes along with celery stalks stuffed with cream cheese lay alongside the entree. He put the plate on the tray and moved it up so it straddled her knees.

"Well? What do you think?" he fished.

"It looks divine." She smiled up at him, loving him with her eyes.

"I'll get mine and we'll eat."

Nelda savored every morsel on her plate and only fleetingly wondered if it was her happiness that made it all seem especially delectable. She chatted easily between bites while she ate her way through one plate of food, and Lute kept up his end of the conversation through two. She marveled that he was able to eat so much and still retain a physique that sported not one ounce of fat. She learned that he had been asked to run for county supervisor but had declined, and that he was on the Fair Board. They shared stories of other holidays, but Nelda carefully steered away from the ones they had shared. She learned of his political inclinations and prejudices, and freely volunteered information about her own. The meal stretched over an hour and a half and ended with pumpkin pie and freshly brewed coffee.

Lute finally carried their dishes to the kitchen.

"Leave them in the sink. I'll do them later," Nelda

called. She was so happy, enraptured with being with him.

"I'll let them soak. We'll have the leftovers for supper."

Nelda closed her eyes tightly and lay back on the couch. He's going to spend the day! What if . . . no, let me not think of anything but being with him.

Lute sprawled in the chair to watch the football game, and Nelda watched him. A thousand memories somersaulted through her mind at the sight of him there, legs stretched out in front of him, eyes half closed. He was a handsome man, charming when he chose to be, with a complete sensual masculinity that any woman would adore. She couldn't blame Miss Home Ec for being wild about him.

She wished with all her heart that she had the right to curl up in his lap as she had done when she was pregnant before. He had loved to caress her taut stomach and feel the movements of their unborn child. During the eight years she was away from him she hadn't forgotten one thing about him. He had lived in her dreams, in her mind, and in her heart. She had looked for his face on every man she had met, gazed into a million laughing eyes, passionate eyes, indifferent eyes, but none of them were Lute's eyes. When she came here she firmly believed it was the only way she could ever expunge him from her heart. She was wrong. He would be in her heart forever. Tears glistened in her eyes and she closed them tightly lest he turn and see them.

The afternoon seemed to pass in the wink of an eye. When darkness came Lute turned on the lamps and let Kelly out to run on the end of his rope. He returned and sat down on the edge of the couch, holding his palm to Nelda's forehead.

"Hungry yet?"

"Are you kidding? I may never eat again!"

"I make a mean turkey sandwich." His eyes dared her to argue, and she laughed.

"Okay. Half a sandwich," she agreed. Her eyes devoured his face.

"I'm going to take your temperature again, and if it's not down, you're going in to see the doctor tomorrow, my girl." His voice threatened, but his hand was gentle against her cheek.

Nelda's temperature was normal, and Lute laughingly took credit for it.

"It was the tender loving care I've given you today."

"It was the aspirin and good food." Nelda's heart was thumping, but she feigned indifference.

She sat on the couch, the blanket across her knees, while her mind strived to sort out Lute's strange behavior. It would be wishful thinking on her part to believe he felt more than pure desire for her. That part of their life had always been perfect. Once he had given her his love, and she had dropped it carelessly. Now all that was left was sexual attraction. They were two lonely people held together by a slender thread of memory . . . youth, young love, and . . . Becky.

She listened to him moving about in the kitchen and thought how easy it would be to marry him again, accepting the desire he offered as a substitute for the love she craved. But by staying with him she would rob him of the chance to find happiness with someone else. The pain of that thought pierced her heart. She hurt so much that it seemed a flood of tears was trapped inside her but she couldn't let them go. Her pride closed the valve, and she smiled brightly when he returned with a tray loaded with the supper they would share.

In spite of her protest he insisted on doing the dishes and leaving them in the rack on the counter. They watched a movie on television, or pretended to. Nelda turned several times to find his eyes on her, and it so unnerved her she hadn't the slightest idea of what was happening on the screen in front of her.

"You don't care for this any more than I do." Lute's

voice cut through her thoughts, and she watched him rise slowly from the chair to turn off the set. He came to the couch and stood looking down at her.

"It wasn't very good," Nelda said in confusion. Her eyes refused to move up to his face. Instead, they focused on the gold watch gleaming against the brown skin of his wrist, the narrow gold band on his finger, and the long legs and slim hips.

He sat down beside her, and Nelda moved until her back was pressed to the end of the couch. Her breathing was still for a second before it quickened again. She could tell he was watching her from under his lashes. He slid a hand along her arm until it reached her shoulder, then followed it to the soft curls around her ears.

"I like your hair like this. You're much prettier than you were at sixteen." She felt his long fingers begin to play with the loose curls. "Some women improve with age, others lose their looks. You're one of those who look more and more beautiful as they get older."

"It was easier to let the natural curl take over," she gasped weakly, drowning in the sensation of his fingertips at her temples.

"Very practical," he agreed, smiling sideways at her. "Talk to me, Nelda. Tell me about these last years."

"You know the important things . . . school, work . . ." She wasn't going to add anything else because there was nothing about those vacant, lonely years that was more important to her than what was happening right now. "What about you? You haven't told me much about yourself," she prodded.

"It didn't seem relevant," he agreed. "I think I can sum it up in a couple of words—work and pleasure. The work was satisfying."

"And the pleasure?" Nelda said, feeling stung. "By that you mean women."

He gave her a sharp look. "Sometimes. When I'd been working full tilt for a long while and I needed to unwind, forget work and other . . . things."

"You must have spiced up the life of the local belles,"
she said wryly.

"They never meant a thing," he said, watching her
face. "I can barely remember most of them. There was
always something missing, however nice they were.
They'd walk out of a room and out of my head at the
same time. But there was one woman always right there
in the middle of my mind, and I couldn't shift *her* out."

"Did you try?" she whispered.

"At first," he admitted softly.

He was looking at her with an expression she knew
all too well. The emotional temperature between them
had risen dramatically, the light, calm companionship
dispelled, the brief truce ruined. There was a sudden,
full, electric tension between them. The lines of his jaw
had grown taut, and his blue eyes were filled with intense
emotion as they focused on her parted lips.

She put up a hand as if to ward off the inevitable, but
it was crushed between them when his mouth came down
hungrily, one of his hands behind her neck forcing her
toward him. His mouth moved fiercely, compellingly,
and Nelda's head began to swim as a heated wave of
excitement clouded her brain.

The onslaught of his mouth softened as he felt her
giving way. His lips moved coaxingly over hers, parting
them, making love to them in a tender, caressing way.
His hand tangled in her hair, his fingers moving through
the dark strands and finding the nape of her neck. She
began to breathe rapidly, aware of his powerful body
pressing her down onto the couch. Her skin felt so hot
she thought she was feverish again, and her bones seemed
to be melting inside her overheated flesh.

Fighting with her wild excitement was the fear of his
learning her secret. She wanted to give in to passion, but
she was afraid. She pushed at his wide shoulders, turning
her head from side to side in an effort to free her mouth.

"Don't, darling. Stop fighting me . . . yourself," Lute said thickly, his mouth a breath away from her own.

"No!" Nelda moaned, shuddering. She was torn between her fascination with the abyss and her fear of it—half of her longing to let go and fall headlong into it, the other half pulling away from the edge as if one step farther would be total destruction.

"Oh, Nelda!" Lute muttered savagely. His face pressed into her neck, his lips trembling as he moved them down her skin.

"Don't," she whispered, her own lips quivering. Her fear was intensified by the hunger she felt in her own body.

"Let me stay, Nelda?" The whispered plea reached her ears from where it was muttered against her neck.

"No, Lute." Desperation was making her angry. It was bad enough to have to fight her own desires without having to fight his, too. "I thank you for bringing the dinner and for the care you've given me today, but I won't pay you by sleeping with you." Oh, no! Had she really said those cruel words?

"Damnit!" The word exploded from him, and she looked quickly into blazing blue eyes. "Is that what you think? I kiss you once and you think I'm so sex-starved that I'd take a woman to bed who's been sick all day, who barely has the strength to make it to the bathroom and back?" He was standing, his eyes raking her. "You can't accept anything without thinking it's got to be paid for. You . . . couldn't accept Becky's death without thinking you were being paid back for marrying me against your parents' wishes. So you cut me off, blocked me out, thinking you'd atone for the *sin!* There's not one ounce of warmth left in your little body."

"No!" she cried, shaking her head. "You don't understand!" The sound of his voice, his unbridled rage, was destroying her.

The ringing of the telephone jarred them into silence,

and Nelda pulled aside the blanket so she could get up. Lute reached it first.

"Hello," his voice barked. "What the hell do you want? Yes, she's here." He shoved the phone into Nelda's hand but stood there, arms folded across his chest, his eyes on her face, while she answered.

"Hello?"

"Nelda, are you all right?" she heard Norris's concerned voice.

"Yes. Are you in Minneapolis?"

"Yes. Marlene and I had Thanksgiving here at the apartment. When are you coming up? Or would you rather not say?"

"Tomorrow?" She made it a question and glanced at Lute.

"Okay. We'll be looking for you. Are things pretty bad for you right now?"

"Yes, but I'm feeling better. Thanks for calling, Norris." She hung up the phone and went back to the living room.

Lute had left the kitchen while she spoke to Norris, but almost immediately he reappeared in the doorway. He had put on his coat and boots. "I'll let Kelly out for you before I go."

"Thank you," Nelda responded weakly, grasping for words that would help her explain, keep him from leaving this way. This is the last time I'll see him, her mind screamed. The very last time, and I've made him hate me!

Lute didn't come inside when he let Kelly back into the kitchen. He closed the door firmly, and moments later Nelda heard the pickup driving off down the lane.

The tight rein she had kept on her emotions broke, her face crumpled, and she gave way to a storm of tears.

Chapter

11

FOR HOURS NELDA lay awake, haunted by Lute's accusations. No matter how often she told herself she was doing the right thing in leaving, she kept thinking of what it would be like to be married to him again. The yearning to be with him throbbed through her veins, and she writhed in agony. She lay on her back and watched the numbers on the digital clock flip, wishing she hadn't had to chase him away. If he'd stayed he would be with her now, and she wouldn't have to feel cold or lonely.

Somehow the night passed, and when she rose from her bed feeling haggard, her spirits at a new low, she looked out the window on a cold, still dawn. *Oh, Lute, I'm leaving, and I can never come back!*

She didn't allow herself the luxury of self-pity for long. She dressed quickly, ate a piece of toast, and drank a glass of milk, thankful she was spared morning sickness. In two hours she had packed her personal things into suitcases, backed the Oldsmobile up to the back door, and, leaving her clothes on hangers, placed them in the trunk on a bedsheet. She was ready.

Leaving the house was a traumatic experience, but leaving it in such disorder was doubly so. The leftover turkey and dressing were in the refrigerator, and half of the pumpkin pie, carefully covered with plastic wrap, sat on the kitchen counter. Boxes she had intended to pack were stacked inside the porch.

Warmly dressed in wool slacks and fur-lined coat, Nelda called Kelly, urged him into the car, locked the door, and drove down the lane to the road without looking back.

The drive to Minneapolis took about three hours on the interstate highway, but those hours seemed like an eternity. She stopped at a rest area and walked Kelly. The cold wind blasting from the north discouraged him from dallying, and soon they were on their way again.

When she reached the suburbs, she stopped at a service station and asked directions to the address Norris had given her. Because she hadn't driven the last time, the exact location of his apartment hadn't stuck in her mind. She planned to check in with Norris and Marlene, let them know she was in town, then go to a motel until her apartment was available.

The wind whipped like a tornado around the apartment building. Nelda struggled against it on her way from the parking area to the door, leaving Kelly in the car barking his dismay at being left alone. She asked the doorman to ring Norris Smithfield's apartment, not caring that he eyed her speculatively.

"Mr. Smithfield will be down, ma'am," the man said, and he resumed his position beside the door, his face expressionless.

Nelda was waiting beside the elevator when the door slid open. She stepped inside and into Norris's arms.

"I had to come!" she blurted. "I couldn't stay one more day."

"I knew something was wrong when I called last night. Marlene's here. She'll take care of you."

The tears spurted. "I don't want to cry, but... I don't know what I'll do about... Kelly."

"Leave Kelly to me." He placed a comforting arm over her shoulders and she leaned against him gratefully.

Marlene was waiting at the apartment door. She held out her arms, and Nelda flew into them.

"I'm sorry. I'm so sorry to be such a... pest."

"Shhh... you're no such thing." Marlene hugged her,

then drew back in alarm and placed her palm against her cheek. "Norris! This girl's burning up. Call Doctor Wilkins!"

"Oh, no, I'm all right."

"You're not all right, Nelda. Give me your coat and sit down." Marlene disappeared and returned with a thermometer. "The doctor will want a reading," she said, placing it in Nelda's mouth.

"I got his office. He'll return the call in a few minutes." Norris came to stand beside Marlene. They looked like anxious parents, and Nelda held out her hand and gratefully clasped Marlene's.

It seemed only seconds until the phone rang. Norris went to answer it, and Marlene took the thermometer, following him into the other room. Nelda rested her throbbing head against the back of the chair.

They returned with their coats in their arms.

"Doctor Wilkins wants you to come in at once, dear," Marlene said gently.

Nelda sat up in alarm. "What's wrong? I can't go and leave Kelly and my things in the car."

"You must go. Norris will get Kelly and take care of everything. He's very capable." She smiled confidently, lovingly, at the man beside her.

"Give me your car keys and the keys to the house in Iowa. I promise it will be taken care of," he instructed Nelda. "Now, get her ready, honey," he said to Marlene. "I'll bring the car to the east entrance."

Several hours later she was tucked into bed in Marlene's spare room, mentally and physically exhausted. The doctor had prescribed a heavy dose of antibiotics, fruit juices, and rest to combat a severe throat infection.

For two days Nelda gave herself up to the luxury of being cared for by Marlene. On the third day she was feeling well enough to plan what she was going to do now that the apartment Marlene had leased for her was available.

"You can't possibly move in until the end of the week."
Marlene set the tray holding the coffee service on the
table between them. "I love having you here. Of course
I'm sorry you were sick, but nevertheless, it gave me a
chance to get to know you better."

"I'll never be able to thank you properly," Nelda said
as Marlene poured the coffee.

The sound of a door closing brought Marlene to her
feet. Her eyes shone when she looked at Nelda, and a
quick smile tilted her lips. "That's Norris. Excuse me
for a moment."

A few minutes later they came into the room, arm in
arm.

"Behold, our little mother is up and around again!"
Norris exclaimed, dropping a kiss onto Nelda's head.

"It's so good to see you. I don't know how I was ever
so fortunate as to meet you two."

"Sheer luck," Norris said with a grin, pulling Marlene
up close to him. "Isn't that right, sweetheart?"

"If you say so, love. Now sit down and let me pour
you some coffee. Even your nose is cold." Her expressive
eyes sought his face, and he playfully rubbed his nose
against her cheek, then placed a quick kiss near her ear.

The communication between them is so wonderful,
so beautiful, Nelda thought with a pang. This is how
love should be!

"Sit down and talk to Nelda while I get a cup," Marlene commanded gently.

Norris smiled at her lovingly and fondled her neck
beneath her hair. "Hurry back," he whispered. His eyes
followed her as she left the room.

"Kelly probably thinks I've deserted him," Nelda said
to fill the void after Marlene left.

"I doubt that. He's fine. I'm sorry we forgot to tell
Marlene about him before she got you an apartment that
doesn't allow pets. I called to see if he'd settled in. The
owner of the kennel said Kelly was unhappy at first, but

his young son has made a point of taking him out and playing with him. He's settling down." Norris pulled a third chair up to the small table and took some papers from his pocket. "I have a few things that need your attention if you feel up to it. Hutchinson called and asked me to stop in. Nothing happens in that area that everyone doesn't know about immediately. When I had the storage company go out to the farm and pack your things, the news spread like a prairie fire. Hutchinson has already had an offer for the farm."

Nelda's hands groped for each other, caught, and held on tightly. This was the beginning of the end. She'd known it had to come, but not this soon!

"He said he had to know right away if you'll accept the offer. I said I'd have you call him in a few days."

"It sounds so . . . final."

"Yes, I know. But if you've really made up your mind to sell, you should act soon. With the interest rate what it is, it won't be easy to find a buyer."

"Did he say who wanted to buy the farm?"

"No. He was very close-mouthed about it, and that's how he should be. Now another thing. Your apartment is ready for you to move into, and I've arranged for maid service. Are you ready for it?"

"I want to keep her a while longer," Marlene protested as she came back into the room. She reached over and clasped Nelda's hand.

"You've done so much already. I'll never be able to repay you."

"Yes you can. You can produce a healthy baby. Norris and I have part interest in him, you know."

Nelda looked out the window quickly so she could blink the mist from her eyes.

"The apartment is only a few blocks away, you two," Norris said patiently, as if talking to children. "And there *is* that instrument called the telephone. You can talk to each other every day."

Once Nelda drank her coffee, she got up from the table to go to her room. Before she could leave, Norris took an envelope from his jacket pocket.

"Lute came to the farm while I was there," he said quietly. "I've never seen a man so angry. He'd have torn my head off if not for the storage company men. There was no reasoning with him at first. He wouldn't believe you weren't coming back. Finally he calmed down and left, but he returned with this envelope. He asked me, quite civilly, to mail it to you after I refused to tell him where you were."

Suddenly heavy with apprehension, Nelda's heart plummeted as she reached with shaking fingers for the long white envelope. She was scarcely aware of saying, "Thank you. Will you excuse me please?"

In her room she looked at the envelope for a long while before she found the courage to open it. This was the first piece of correspondence she had received from Lute since before their divorce, but she recognized the handwriting. He always made a printed *N* when he wrote her name in script. When they were first married he used to leave little love notes on the table before he left for work in the pre-dawn hours.

With her bottom lip caught firmly between her teeth to stop its trembling, she slipped a finger beneath the sealed flap and took out the single sheet of white paper with the letterhead SWEET CLOVER FARMS, INC., Lute Hanson, Owner.

The text of the letter jumped at her in a bold script. It was brief, formal, and agonizing.

Dear Nelda:

Hutchinson tells me you've put the farm up for sale. As your land adjoins mine and I'm interested in acquiring more acreage, I've made him an offer to be relayed to you. I am not, however, interested

in the house, only the land it sits on. If I acquire
the property, I will most likely demolish the house
and till the ground. I'm aware the house may have
sentimental value for you, but I can't afford sen-
timentality. It doesn't put dollars in the bank. I'm
sure you can understand my position.

Lute
P.S. You and Smithfield should hitch well together.

Nelda sat for a long moment looking at the letter in
her hand. She didn't cry—she was beyond tears—but
she shivered uncontrollably. What was wrong with her
that she could love this cold, hard, unfeeling man? She
wanted the tender, affectionate Lute of long ago and the
warm love they had shared when they were young. No,
she didn't want to love this Lute . . . yet she had to face
the fact that she had more than slightly contributed to
what her gentle boy-husband had become. And she had
to face the fact that underneath his veneer of hostility,
he was still the same Lute she would always love.

Nelda was alone too much now. It was the middle of
December, only ten days before Christmas. She forced
herself to eat three small, well-balanced meals every day,
and every afternoon she found new routes to walk ap-
proximately two miles. On the very coldest days she
walked the six long blocks to the indoor shopping mall
and paced briskly up and down the enormous corridor.
The rest of her time was spent working on designs for
her block prints. She had set up a small table beside
the living room windows, and she sat for hours with
a razor knife, cutting film stencils to adhere to the
silk screen she would use to make her prints.

She missed Kelly dreadfully, but she knew that for
now she had to abide by this apartment building's rules.
Come spring she'd look for a new home. She felt better

about leaving him at the kennel after she and Norris drove out to visit him. He was happy to see her, leaping and bounding in his excitement, but when the owner's young son came to play ball with him, he wagged his tail in a goodbye and trotted off for the action. He seemed well adjusted—better adjusted, in fact, than Nelda herself felt.

Fortunately, Marlene was becoming the mother-sister Nelda had never had. Her own mother had been a woman of strict self-discipline, who had loved her in her own way but expected her to conform without question to what society expected of her. After Nelda had become pregnant and married Lute, the breach between mother and daughter had widened until they were virtual strangers to each other. Marlene, on the other hand, was warm, affectionate, and understanding, and Nelda thought it no wonder that Norris loved her so much.

Time was sometimes heavy, and certain days felt a week long. The odd jobs around the apartment, the light housework—she'd dispensed with the maid service—the small amount of cooking and shopping didn't take much time at all. She walked her two miles a day religiously, but it wasn't always enjoyable to walk alone. She was noticing that about a lot of things—an evening at the theater, an outing to the museum—all would have been much more fun with . . . someone to share the experience. She was beginning to realize the dangers of a solitary profession. She read, worked, drove out to see Kelly, visited with Marlene, and at times she still wanted to scream. She grew tense and strained and was consumed with guilt over selling the farm. The thought of her Grandma's beloved house being torn down, the lumber being loaded into trucks and hauled away, was a constant pain in her heart. It would have been better, she thought, if the tornado had blown it away the day it took the roof off the garage.

Two days after she'd moved into the apartment she

had phoned Mr. Hutchinson and told him to accept Lute's offer.

"We don't need to be hasty, Mrs. Hanson. Someone else is interested, too," he'd argued.

"I don't care who else is interested," she'd snapped. "Sell it to Lute Hanson for whatever he offers." She hung up the phone and wondered at her irritability.

A week later she called back to ask if the deal had been finalized.

"Not yet, but if you leave a number where I can reach you, I'll call you as soon as the papers are ready for you to sign."

Nelda reluctantly gave him her phone number. "When you're ready, I'll meet you somewhere. I want this over with as soon as possible." She knew the lawyer was puzzled by her unusual behavior, but she was past caring what he thought. Her only worry was that when she did meet him she wouldn't be so far along in her pregnancy that her coat couldn't hide her condition.

There was nothing to do but wait. Wait for Hutchinson to call, wait for Marlene or Norris to visit, wait for her appointments with Doctor Wilkins. The shopping mall was now always crowded with holiday shoppers. Christmas music filled every corner of the vast complex. People rushed in and out of the stores, their arms loaded with packages, their faces lit with smiles as the holiday spirit prevailed everywhere. Everywhere except in Nelda's heart; she prayed that this time of the year, so special for families, would hurry and be over.

In the florist shop she wired flowers to her father and stepmother in Florida and on impulse sent a similar gift to Rhetta and Gary. For Marlene she bought something special—a thin gold bracelet with a small whistle charm. On a card she wrote, "If you ever need me, whistle and I'll come, even if I'm on the other side of the world." For Norris she bought a box of his favorite cigars and a limited edition novel by an author she knew he admired. In less than an hour her Christmas shopping was done.

On days when the weather was bad and the sidewalks icy, she didn't leave the apartment—Norris and Marlene had warned that they'd have her head if she risked a fall.

This had been one of those days. When the telephone rang she moved listlessly to answer it. She hoped if it was Norris he'd volunteer some news about Lute, because she would never ask. At times she was consumed with jealousy thinking about Lute with another woman.

"Hello?"

A few seconds of silence preceded the announcement, "This is Lute."

Nelda felt her blood go cold. Her hand gripped the phone until her fingers ached. She was too stunned to speak, and all in one moment she experienced a great surge of love and fright.

"How . . . did you get my number?" she whispered haltingly.

"It wasn't easy. Smithfield refused to tell me where you were. I was in Hutchinson's office when he pulled out a pile of papers from your file, and this number was written on the top of one of them. I jotted it down." Her heart throbbed painfully while she listened to the familiar voice. "I just want to talk to you for a little while. Are you all right?"

"Yes, I'm fine." Her heart rose in her throat.

"I just want to talk you," he repeated, "and make sure you're well." The humble tone of his voice tore at her very soul.

"I'm okay," she mumbled, trying to sound convincing.

"I could tell by the area code that you're in the Twin Cities. Are you working on the big decorating job you were telling me about?"

"I'm just doing the preliminary work here. I'll probably start the actual work . . . in a few months." Nelda dropped down onto a chair, her legs suddenly weak.

There was silence on the other end of the line. Presently he asked, "Are you going back to New York?"

"Yes."

"When? When are you leaving?" There seemed to be a darting note of pain in his voice, but Nelda was swallowing the sobs in her throat and couldn't be certain it wasn't just her own hopes misleading her.

"I'm . . . not sure," she murmured raggedly.

"Did you get my letter?"

For a minute she couldn't speak, and when she did her voice was a pathetic croak. "About . . . Grandma's house?"

"About my buying the farm. I've signed the papers and given Hutchinson a down payment."

"Then . . . it's settled. You'll tear the house down," she acknowledged with difficulty.

"No, darling. I won't tear it down. I'm sorry I ever said that. I wanted to hurt you. I know you love that old place. It was small and petty of me to make you think I was going to wreck it." He said the words quietly and sincerely.

Comprehension seeped into her consciousness. *Darling*. He'd said *darling*. She struggled for something to say.

"Did you hear me, Nelda? I won't tear it down."

"I heard you," she whispered hoarsely.

"It's just a week until Christmas. Will you spend it alone?"

"Oh, no," she said lightly. "I have friends here."

"I've been invited to Rhetta and Gary's. Rhetta is planning a big New Year's Eve party, too. Gary has gotten the bug to raise Arabian horses and wants me to go partners with him on a registered stallion."

"Are you going to?" It seemed unreal that she and

Lute could be having this casual conversation.

"I'm thinking about it. It would mean going to a lot of horse shows and fairs."

"I saw a horse show in Madison Square Garden once. The animals were beautiful, but I didn't know the difference between an Arabian and a Tennessee Walker unless I looked at the program." She was stammering for words to say.

"Do you like horses?"

She hesitated. "Yes, though they're awfully big. Dogs are more my size."

"How does Kelly like living in the city again?"

"He's in a kennel. I can't keep him with me here."

"You could have left him with me." There was a long pause while he waited for her to respond. When she didn't, he said, "I want to call you again." His voice was almost a whisper.

"No! Don't call again. It's best for us to make a clean break, Lute. It was nice of you to call and ask about me. I'm glad it was you who bought Grandpa's farm. 'Bye, Lute." She got up from the chair, holding the phone away from her ear as she went to lay it back in the cradle.

"Nelda—" His voice reached her before the connection was broken.

She went into the bathroom, closed the door, and turned the water on in the bathtub. If Lute called back, she didn't want to hear the phone ring.

That night she lay awake for hours, staring into the darkness, her thoughts in a riot of confusion. Why had Lute called? Could he still be a little in love with her? No, she told herself sternly, that was wishful thinking. Even if he were . . . no, she'd vowed to stay out of his life.

The next evening Marlene and Norris took her out to dinner. Norris had spent the week in Chicago and had come back to the Twin Cities to have a pre-Christmas holiday with Marlene. Marlene would spend Christmas day with her daughter and husband at the care facility.

Nelda didn't mention Lute's call. The sound of his voice had affected her so deeply she tried not to think about it.

It was ten o'clock when she let herself back into the apartment. She looked accusingly at the telephone, as if it should tell her whether or not it had rung, then started preparations for bed. She was wearing clothes with looser waistbands now. She had invested in several pairs of warm slacks, a couple pairs of jeans, and a few tops. Most of her sweaters would stretch enough to get her through the winter.

It had become a ritual to undress and look at herself in the long bedroom mirror before she put on her flannel nightgown. She did this now, shook her head in disbelief, and rubbed her palms over her protruding abdomen.

"Baby, Baby! If you don't stop growing so fast, you're going to be big enough for school when you get here. But I want you big and healthy . . . like your Daddy." As if in response, a small movement fluttered against her hand. She caught her breath. This wondrous thing was happening, and she had no one to share it with—no one to laugh because she waddled like a duck, or to rub her aching back, or to look forward to the day her son arrived. She looked down at her altered shape. She wished for happier circumstances for her baby's arrival into the world, but whatever happened, she wanted this baby too much to care. Only today Doctor Wilkins had said these months of her pregnancy should be carefree. Carefree? What in the world was that?

She was standing in front of the mirror when the phone rang. Her eyes darted to the instrument on the table beside the bed. It rang twice before she moved, and that was to pick up her nightgown and slip it over her head, as if standing naked while the phone was ringing was somehow indecent.

Would Lute be calling this late? It could be Norris or

Marlene, and if she didn't answer they would be worried. They might even make a trip back over to her building. If it was Lute she didn't have to talk to him—she could hang up. After this momentary deliberation she reached for the phone.

"Hello?"

"Nelda, I've been calling all evening." Lute! She didn't answer, couldn't answer. "Nelda, please don't hang up." His voice rasped queerly.

"What do you want? If it's something about the farm, you could call Mr. Hutchinson." Her voice was soft and more controlled than she expected it to be.

"It's nothing about the farm. I just wanted to talk to you and see how you're doing."

"It's nice of you to be so concerned, but—"

"Nelda! Don't hang up!"

"Lute, we've nothing to talk about." She wrenched out the lie, forcing herself to remember her resolution not to get involved in Lute's life again.

"I wish you didn't feel that way." There was a kind of sadness in his voice, and her heart beat faster.

"Why now, Lute?" she questioned, trying to sound annoyed, while her heart cried, *Why now, Lute, when I'm trying so hard to set you free...?* "We had plenty of opportunity to talk when I was at the farm. The only times you called me then were to chew me out about something. What have I done wrong this time?" she demanded, almost convincing herself with her assumed anger.

"You did nothing wrong and I did everything. I loused up. My only defense is that it was a shock to see you again. I never thought you'd come back." His voice sounded haunted and hurt and tired and sad.

"What do you want to talk about, Lute? I'm tired and want to go to bed." With you . . . her heart finished the statement. Nelda sank down on the bed. You crazy fool, she told herself. You're asking for another sleepless night.

He hesitated. "Are you seeing a lot of Smithfield?"

A short expulsion of breath escaped her lips. She moved to slam the phone onto the hook in self-righteous outrage, but caught herself. After all, wouldn't it be easier if he thought that? Maybe he'd stop torturing her with his confusing concern.

"What business is it of yours who I see? I see a lot of men! I like sex, Lute. I try to get a man lined up in every state. I've got several in New York, one in Florida, Norris in Minnesota. Would you like to be my man in Iowa? Is that what you wanted to hear, Lute?" She sniffed back tears and said, "What else do you want to know?"

"Nothing, darling. I'm sorry I asked. But, damnit, it's been tearing me apart. Let me come see you, Nelda."

"No, Lute. It's too late. I'm not the kind of woman you want. I . . . don't know the first thing about freezing corn, or about . . . soybeans, and I'd be no good trying to cook for a bunch of threshers . . . you know . . . I can't cook!"

"Farmers' wives don't cook for threshers any more. I do my own threshing, and if I have extra men to feed, I have a catering service bring something out," he said reasonably.

"Why are you telling me this, Lute? I have my career, just as you have yours, and they're miles apart."

"Maybe they don't have to be, darling. Let me come see you. Just listen to me for a minute. Eight years is a long time. I thought I was over you, but there wasn't a time when I couldn't picture your face in my mind. Then you came back more beautiful than ever, sweeter to hold, and a highly intelligent woman with a successful career to boot. How could an Iowa farmer hope to touch that?" His voice grew husky. "After I . . . lost you and Becky, I made up my mind I'd never marry again, or have another child. Then I met you at the cemetery, and I guess I did resent your power to make me mindless when I was with you."

Why is he telling me this now, when it's too late, her mind screamed.

"Why are you telling me this now, Lute?" she whispered through trembling lips.

"Why? Because you're the most beautiful, most incredibly sexy woman I've ever known. Because...oh, Nelda, don't make me beg to see you!"

She didn't have to pretend anger and hurt any more. A tight pain was squeezing her chest. *Incredibly sexy.* That was all she meant to him!

"If you're looking for a regular bed partner, Lute, I'm sure Miss Home Ec will oblige. I'm not available!" she shouted wildly. She slammed the phone down, only to pick it up again when the connection was broken and let it fall to the floor.

She flung herself down on the bed, fighting for control. What a complete fool she was! She had dared to hope he was going to say he loved her still. But he only wanted to go to bed with her!

A wave of sickness rose in her, and she struggled to swallow it down. Well, hadn't she wanted to get away from him, to set him free? This should make it a lot easier, shouldn't it? But it didn't...

Chapter
12

CHRISTMAS EVE.

Nelda had faced it with dread, knowing that she would be spending it alone. Marlene had gone to visit her husband, and Norris had flown to California to spend a few hours with his daughters. The two gaily wrapped packages on the table beside the miniature tree Marlene had insisted on setting up for her were from them. Tomorrow she would call her father and thank him for his check, telling him she'd bought an expensive peignoir or some other frivolous thing, when in truth the check was still in the envelope.

She had spent other Christmases alone, but they had been less lonely. She found herself missing the hurry-scurry of New York streets, office celebrations, the apartment building where everyone sang out, "Merry Christmas!" to each other. She thought about calling Rhetta and Gary, to wish them happy holidays, but they were too close to Lute. If he and Janythe Graham were spending the holidays together, she didn't want to know about it.

It had been a week since Lute called, and she could still hear the sound of his voice in the middle of the night. He had humbled himself and begged to see her. She was sure his pride was wounded when she refused. He wouldn't call her again.

Nelda sat down in the chair beside the floor-to-ceiling windows and looked out over the city. It was a Christmas-card scene. Large, fluffy snowflakes were falling softly, last-minute shoppers were hurrying home. It would soon be dark, and Christmas lights would come on all over the city.

She was a good four months pregnant now, and her swelling stomach tallied with the date. It was nicely rounded, and she patted it with a warm little smile.

"Merry Christmas, Baby."

She fought back thoughts of Lute, Becky, and Christmases past and found herself humming "Silent Night" as if to comfort the small life growing inside her.

The bell on the intercom sounded, startling her. The room was almost dark, and she fumbled for the lamp switch and pulled the drapes before she answered.

"Yes?"

"Someone is here with a package from Mr. Smithfield and insists on delivering it personally. Shall I let him come up?"

"I guess so," she said tiredly.

She turned on more lights, suddenly feeling less lonely. Norris had thoughtfully arranged a surprise, knowing the evening would be long for her.

The soft chimes of her doorbell sounded. She opened the door and froze, stunned. Lute! The collar of his fur-lined coat was turned up, and flakes of snow were melting on his hatless head. Nelda noticed all this in a mere second before she closed her eyes. She opened them again to see if what she thought she saw was real. His face looked tired and thin, his eyes quiet and pleading. No, they couldn't be pleading with her. The last time he had looked at her they'd chilled her with their coldness. Now she felt as if her insides were melting in their warmth. He pushed the door open with one hand. By the time she came out of shock he was inside the room.

He stood silent, immobile, waiting. Slowly Nelda began to back away, a few steps at a time, until her back came up against the railing that separated the entrance from the living room.

"Nelda?" he spoke at last. "I'm sorry if I surprised you. I . . ."

Her chin trembled. Why was he here, she asked herself, staring at him. Had he come about the farm? Had he brought papers for her to sign? Thoughts swirled round and round in her fogged brain.

"What do you want?" she impelled her voice to ask.

"Why are you looking at me like that?" he responded. She saw his eyes flick over her and come to rest on her stomach. "Nelda! My God, Nelda, you're . . ."

She turned her back on him and started across the room. He closed the gap between them in one long stride, and his hands on her upper arms pulled her to a stop and back against him. The cold leather of his coat sent a chill through her.

"Why didn't you tell me?" he grated.

Not, *Is it mine?* Just, *Why didn't you tell me?* She closed her eyes tightly.

"It isn't yours!" she lied.

"Liar!" he said tightly.

"No!" She twisted away from him. "The baby is my responsibility," she tried next.

"Ours!" he contradicted. "Why?" he muttered in a hoarse, thickened voice. "Why? Why would you deny me my child? You had to know I'd want it."

"The baby, but not me. And we're a package deal. I knew you'd marry me anyway if you knew, but I don't want you to. I couldn't bear that same situation all over again. We'd be back to square one, with you caught in the same trap with the wrong woman. So this time I'll raise my child alone, surrounded with love, not resentment." She paused, summoning the courage she'd need to say the words she knew she had to say. "Please go," she whispered.

There was silence behind her. She held her breath, waiting to hear the door open and close.

"Nelda Elaine," he rasped, "you sweet little fool. Don't

you know you mean more to me than anything in the world? Why do you think I'm here? I didn't even know about the baby."

She gasped, trying to register his words. Her mind protested that maybe sheer physical desire had motivated his visit.

"No, Lute, I can't believe that. I'm not suited for your kind of life—you've told me that over and over again. No matter how hard I tried these past few months, you were just waiting for me to fail, waiting for me to give up like I had eight years ago. You'll never forgive me for wanting to do something of my own."

"We're not kids any more, Nelda," he said quietly.

"Please go," she whispered again, practically gasping from the pain of saying the words.

"No. I'll not leave you to have my baby alone." He was behind her again, and this time when he drew her back against him, it was his warm, hard chest covered only by a shirt that she felt. "This time it will be different, darling." She could feel his lips against her hair. "I'll share you with a career if that's what you want. We don't even have to live on the farm. We'll live wherever you'll be happy. I love you," he said, and she thought she heard desperation in his voice. "I always have."

Was it really Lute speaking these words? "How can you be so sure the baby is yours?" she protested feebly, no longer certain what she was fighting.

He turned her in his arms. She could see the shadow of pain his eyes. He had lost weight, and his leaner face was more forceful than ever.

"There's not a doubt in my mind that this baby is mine. Ours. And it needs two parents, Nelda. You and me. I need you, darling, and I hope you need me."

"I always have," the words broke from her lips.

A dam had broken inside her, and she began crying uncontrollably. She did need him, desperately, and yet she was frightened of the future. His arms enfolded her slowly, as if he was afraid she would push him away. She turned her face into his shoulder and leaned against him wearily. His arms tightened and they stood there, pressed together, not speaking, merely drinking in the closeness of each other's bodies. She put her arms around him, her hands feeling his comforting strength, gratefully stroking the broad back. He buried his face in her hair, kissing it, murmuring her name softly.

"Just hold me, Lute," she whispered, still unable to believe what was happening.

"Sweetheart, I've been through hell and back these past few weeks. I couldn't face spending the rest of my life without you. I let you get away from me one time— I'll never let it happen again." He tried to kiss the wetness from her eyes. "We'll make it work, darling," he told her huskily.

She looked up, smiling through her tears. "I just couldn't come to you and say, 'Look, we've done it again.' I knew you'd want to marry me, and I was afraid it would be the same as before. I couldn't have lived with knowing that the reason we'd married was because I was pregnant again."

"Silly woman! I wanted to marry you more than anything in the world, just as I do now—as I wanted to do before I knew you were pregnant. I came here to bring you this," and he eased away from her enough to produce a small box from his pocket.

Then his mouth closed over hers gently and Nelda stopped smiling, but inside her the laughter spread out, dancing through her blood. The kiss was long and sweet and conveyed a meaning far too poignant for mere words. Still holding her in a kiss, he backed up and sat down in the big chair, pulling her into his arms and settling her onto his lap, his hands roughly tender. He leaned back, cuddled her against him, and lifted her arm to encircle his neck.

"I wanted to do this on Thanksgiving, but I didn't

dare. I promised myself I'd never let the chance slip by again. I love you, Nelda Hanson with an *o*," he said fiercely, looking deeply into her eyes. His own were unexpectedly vulnerable, and they melted Nelda's heart. "Aren't you going to open your present?" he prompted with sudden boyish enthusiasm. "It's the engagement ring I couldn't afford for you the last time," he whispered, his voice deep with emotion.

"I love you, Lute Hanson with an *o*. I love you in more ways than I knew a woman could love. I fell in love with a boy, and he grew into a man. My love has grown, too." She put a finger over his mouth when he opened it to speak. "Hush and listen. I always felt so damn inadequate for you. You knew exactly what you wanted to do, and I still had so much to prove to myself. With you working so hard, at times I felt like a millstone around your neck. Then, when Becky was gone, and you agreed to the divorce, I figured you felt your obligation to me was over."

"Obligation? You crazy kid! I *loved* you—I love you now. I've always loved you. I thought you were ashamed of what I'd chosen to do with my life, and when you left, I thought you wanted to be free of me. I worked my ass off to be the best farmer I could be, to prove to myself I wasn't a total failure. I never thought I'd have the chance to prove it to you. Then one day you came back, and my stupid pride made me act the fool!"

She put her fingers over his lips again, "Hush . . . and kiss me."

After securing the diamond ring on the proper finger of her left hand, he readily obliged her.

His smile was ineffably tender as he stroked her cheek. "Merry Christmas, darling," he whispered. Then gently, with his palm beneath her chin, he lifted her face to his and kissed her again, softly at first, and then harder, his arms holding her close, his mouth clinging tightly to hers. He held her snugly against him for a long while, and they kissed slowly, hauntingly, as if to make up for the years without love. She knew they couldn't have those years back, but they had now and the future.

"When is the baby due?" he asked between nuzzling kisses.

"The last of May."

"Good." His hand moved up under her loose blouse, his fingers gently touching her stomach.

"What do you mean, 'Good'?"

"I'll have you all to myself for the rest of the winter. I'll make you eat good meals, take vitamins—"

"I'll be as big as a cow!"

"Not quite," he said, laughing softly. "But that reminds me—spring is birthing season on the farm, too. I'm going to be a busy man."

"Oh, Lute, I've loved you for so long. I tried to break the bond, but it was too tough for me," she admitted with a sigh.

"I'm so glad it was!" His lips pressed against hers possessively, and the hand under her blouse caressed the warm flesh of her rounded abdomen and moved up to cup one unrestrained breast. "A perfect fit," he murmured, squeezing gently. "Your little body is so neat and tight. When I get a chance, I'm going to spank that little behind of yours for leaving without a word. I thought I was making progress Thanksgiving Day, and then ...zoom...you were gone. I almost went out of my mind."

Laughter and happiness bubbled up within her, and, putting both arms about his neck, she pressed her parted lips to his.

"I never thought I'd be this happy again," she exclaimed. "Oh, Lute, it's Christmas Eve. Come, I want to show you something." She got up off his lap and drew him up beside her. "Turn out the light. I want to give you diamonds, too." When the room was dark, she pulled back the drapes and the lighted city sparkled before them. "Merry Christmas, darling."

"Merry Christmas." He pulled her around in front of him and wrapped his arms around her. He bent his knees slightly and settled her rounded bottom tightly against the front of his corded jeans.

"Hmmmmm..." he murmured. "Hmmm, you feel so good."

"Oh, Lute. I don't have any other present for you."

He lifted his head from her neck. "What do you call this?" His large hands cupped her rounded stomach.

They had not been in bed very long—just long enough to make love. They lay face to face, legs entwined as intimately as their arms, lips touching, sharing the same pillow and the same breath.

"Sweetheart, I don't expect you to give up your career; that is, if you can figure out some way to have some time for me. You've worked up a reputation for being good in your field and—"

Nelda put her fingers over his lips. "Is there room in that big old farmhouse for a studio for me? I can do most of what I want to do right there at home with an occasional visit back east. From now on my place is with my family. Oh, it sounds so good to say that!" she exulted.

"Beautiful, adorable, sexy woman! Even at sixteen—when you were skinny and had that long hair you wanted so desperately to be straight—you were sexy," he murmured, kissing her nose while his hands caressed her back and pulled her taut rounded stomach closer into the hollow of his.

"How did you find me?" For the first time the question came to her mind. "I thought I had all the bases covered."

"Smithfield told me." He pulled her over until she rested on top of him.

"Norris? He promised!"

"When I answered the phone, he said something like, 'Damnit, are you in love with Nelda or not?' And I said, 'It's none of your damn business how I feel about her, but I'll tell you anyway. She was my first love, my only love, and if you don't treat her right I'll rearrange your face!' He laughed at me and called me all kinds of a fool, then he gave me your address and told me how to get past the doorman. He said I was on my own, that I'd have one slim chance, and that I'd better not fumble the ball."

"He's been a wonderful friend. He's not at all the playboy everyone thinks he is. Wait until you meet Marlene, the woman he loves, and you'll see what I mean." She ran her fingers down his sides from his armpits to as far as as she could reach along his lean thighs.

"You'll get in trouble doing that," he whispered after a hastily indrawn breath. "What do you think you're doing?"

"Seducing you," she said cheerfully, kissing a hard nipple buried in the soft down on his chest, her heart feeling full but light.

He lifted her chin and kissed her with what felt like all the pent-up longing of years, and she returned the force of his kiss, holding nothing back. His hand covered one breast, his fingers stroking her nipple until it was hard, his lips following to bring more joy. She felt an urgency build in her and a stirring in him. His hands searched her smooth flesh and finally moved downward until he found what he sought. The years of pain melted away, and her body came alive and sang for him as it had sung when they were young. But in her ears the song was even sweeter, deeper, richer, than ever before.

"Will our son mind?" he whispered huskily. "Selfish little begger has you all the time," he pouted.

"Don't blame me—I didn't put him there," she whispered, laughing softly and blindly seeking his mouth with hers. "But I don't think he'll mind at all."

In late May Lute brought Nelda and Scott Edward home from the hospital. She saw with joy that the bridal wreath lining the drive leading to the farmhouse was in full bloom, as were the peonies in front of the house. Kelly was waiting at the end of the drive and ran alongside the car, barking his greeting. Lute's mother had come over from Nelda's old farmhouse, where she had been living since the New Year, to see Nelda and the new baby. She stood anxiously beside the back door. It still amazed Nelda how readily all of Mrs. Hanson's animosity had faded in the face of her son's obvious happiness.

"He's beautiful!" she exclaimed, reaching greedily for her grandchild. "Look at that blond hair! I'm afraid he's going to look like you, Lute."

"Poor little mite," Nelda teased. "One strike against him already."

Lute tweaked her nose. "And what's wrong with a boy looking like his Pa?" He put his arms around her, his blue eyes shining. "You feel so damn good," he whispered in her ear. "I've missed having you here. You'll have to have the next baby right here at home, and I'll call Gary over to tend you."

"You crazy man, you!" She locked her arms about his neck. "I love you, and I've missed you, too."

They followed the proud grandmother upstairs to the room that had been furnished as a nursery. A new, obviously handmade mobile of small, colorful animals hung over the crib.

"I was reading that it helps a baby to focus its eyes at an early age," Lute said sheepishly. "I've hung it just the right distance."

Nelda laughed. "How did you manage to get the crops

in while doing all this heavy reading—and carpentry?" she asked, indicating the tiny wooden animals dancing over the crib.

He produced a worn paperback from his pocket. "Odd minutes at the end of a row, and odd evenings when you've been working in your studio. I thought I should learn all these things. Bringing up a child isn't easy, and we must do things right."

Nelda sat down in a chair and reached for her son. "It's time for his feeding," she explained to an understanding Mrs. Hanson. The older woman bustled out, saying she'd fix some lunch for the nursing mother.

The baby fastened its tiny blond head to Nelda's breast, and she inhaled deeply as she felt the tiny sharp pain that gave way to such pleasure.

Lute knelt down beside them, staring with fascination. "He reminds me of the little piglets we have in the barn," he said, watching his son's face turn pink from exertion. "Why, he's the greediest little begger I've ever seen!"

"He enjoys his meals, just like his father," Nelda said, gently hugging the precious bundle to her.

"I can't say as I blame him," Lute said agreeably, his eyes lingering on the white globe of his wife's breast. "I love you, Mrs. Hanson with an *o*," he said in a husky, reverent voice.

Nelda had never seen such a tender expression on his face, nor so much love in his eyes. An emotional whisper was all she could manage.

"I love you, too, Mr. Hanson."

____ 06195-6 **SHAMROCK SEASON #35** Jennifer Rose
____ 06304-5 **HOLD FAST TIL MORNING #36** Beth Brookes
____ 06282-0 **HEARTLAND #37** Lynn Fairfax
____ 06408-4 **FROM THIS DAY FORWARD #38** Jolene Adams
____ 05968-4 **THE WIDOW OF BATH #39** Anne Devon
____ 06400-9 **CACTUS ROSE #40** Zandra Colt
____ 06401-7 **PRIMITIVE SPLENDOR #41** Katherine Swinford
____ 06424-6 **GARDEN OF SILVERY DELIGHTS #42** Sharon Francis
____ 06521-8 **STRANGE POSSESSION #43** Johanna Phillips
____ 06326-6 **CRESCENDO #44** Melinda Harris
____ 05818-1 **INTRIGUING LADY #45** Daphne Woodward
____ 06547-1 **RUNAWAY LOVE #46** Jasmine Craig
____ 06423-8 **BITTERSWEET REVENGE #47** Kelly Adams
____ 06541-2 **STARBURST #48** Tess Ewing
____ 06540-4 **FROM THE TORRID PAST #49** Ann Cristy
____ 06544-7 **RECKLESS LONGING #50** Daisy Logan
____ 05851-3 **LOVE'S MASQUERADE #51** Lillian Marsh
____ 06148-4 **THE STEELE HEART #52** Jocelyn Day
____ 06422-X **UNTAMED DESIRE #53** Beth Brookes
____ 06651-6 **VENUS RISING #54** Michelle Roland
____ 06595-1 **SWEET VICTORY #55** Jena Hunt
____ 06575-7 **TOO NEAR THE SUN #56** Aimée Duvall
____ 05625-1 **MOURNING BRIDE #57** Lucia Curzon
____ 06411-4 **THE GOLDEN TOUCH #58** Robin James
____ 06596-X **EMBRACED BY DESTINY #59** Simone Hadary
____ 06660-5 **TORN ASUNDER #60** Ann Cristy
____ 06573-0 **MIRAGE #61** Margie Michaels
____ 06650-8 **ON WINGS OF MAGIC #62** Susanna Collins

All of the above titles are $1.75 per copy

All of the above titles are $1.75 per copy

WHAT READERS SAY ABOUT
SECOND CHANCE AT LOVE BOOKS

"Your books are the greatest!"
—M. N., Carteret, New Jersey*

"I have been reading romance novels for quite some time, but the SECOND CHANCE AT LOVE books are the most enjoyable."
—P. R., Vicksburg, Mississippi*

"I enjoy SECOND CHANCE [AT LOVE] more than any books that I have read and I do read a lot."
—J. R., Gretna, Louisiana*

"For years I've had my subscription in to Harlequin. Currently there is a series called Circle of Love, but you have them all beat."
—C. B., Chicago, Illinois*

"I really think your books are exceptional . . . I read Harlequin and Silhouette and although I still like them, I'll buy your books over theirs. SECOND CHANCE [AT LOVE] is more interesting and holds your attention and imagination with a better story line . . ."
—J. W., Flagstaff, Arizona*

"I've read many romances, but yours take the 'cake'!"
—D. H., Bloomsburg, Pennsylvania*

"Have waited ten years for *good* romance books. Now I have them."
—M. P., Jacksonville, Florida*

*Names and addresses available upon request